"What ... *last night...*

"It didn't... I didn't... I thought you were Chris... I was dreaming about him and when... You must have known that I would never... That..."

Poppy stopped abruptly as she saw the dangerous warning expression on James's face, her stomach dropping sickeningly as she realized how angry he was.

"Go on," he invited her softly. "You were saying that you thought I was Chris, that you were dreaming about Chris, but you weren't asleep when we made love, were you, Poppy? You knew very well who it was, who was holding you...touching you, pleasuring you," he told her tauntingly, "even if you do claim now that you wanted it to be my brother...."

Dear Reader,

What is more natural than a bride wanting her closest friends also to find happiness in love? For Sally, this means tricking three of her wedding guests into catching her bouquet! Three women, each very different, but all with their own reasons for never wanting to marry. That is why they agree to a pact to stay single, but just how long will it take for the bouquet to begin its magic?

Penny Jordan has worked *her* magic on these three linked stories. One of Harlequin's most successful and popular authors, she has written three compelling romances—all complete stories in themselves—that follow the lives—and loves—of Claire, Poppy and Star. *Best Man to Wed?* is Poppy's story. She is the close cousin of Sally's new husband, and she is devastated at having lost the man *she* wanted to marry—and Poppy hardly needs the best man telling her to grow up and find herself a real man!

THE BRIDE'S BOUQUET—three women make a pact to stay single, but one by one they fall, seduced by the power of love

Look out for Star's story in

Too Wise to Wed? July 1997
Harlequin Presents #1895

PENNY JORDAN

Best Man to Wed?

Harlequin Books

TORONTO • NEW YORK • LONDON
AMSTERDAM • PARIS • SYDNEY • HAMBURG
STOCKHOLM • ATHENS • TOKYO • MILAN
MADRID • WARSAW • BUDAPEST • AUCKLAND

ISBN 0-373-11889-9

BEST MAN TO WED?

First North American Publication 1997.

Copyright © 1996 by Penny Jordan.

This edition published by arrangement with Harlequin Books S.A.

Printed in U.S.A.

POPPY CARLTON stared mournfully across the now empty garden, furiously trying to blink away her tears.

It seemed only yesterday that she and Chris used to play here. She had been happy then, never thinking that there might come a day when she and her cousin would not be so close, a day when someone else, another woman, would become the main focus of his life, his time, his future, his love.

Fresh tears brimmed and welled over. Poppy dashed them away with the back of her hand.

She had known for months, of course, that Chris and Sally were going to marry, but somehow, until the actual day of the wedding, she had gone on... What? Hoping that he would change his mind, that he would look at her, love her as a woman and not just as a cousin?

'Your turn next,' Chris had laughed affectionately at her as she had leapt forward with Claire, Sally's stepmother, and Star, her closest friend, to catch the bouquet which Sally had dropped as she'd slipped on the stairs.

Her turn next. Impossible. She would *never* marry now. How could she when the man she loved, the only man she had ever loved or ever would love, was lost to her?

And of course her other cousin, James, Chris's elder brother and best man, would have to have witnessed the whole thing—the falling bouquet, her instinctive attempt to save it along with Claire and Star, and, worst of all, the compassion and, humiliatingly, the relief as well in Chris's eyes as he had made some cumbersome joke about her at least waiting until he and Sally had returned from their honeymoon before fulfilling the traditional prophecy that went with the catching of the bride's bouquet.

Oh, yes, James had seen all of that and predictably had made no attempt to spare her the full force of his cynical denunciation of her feelings as he had told her, 'Grow up, Poppy; grow up and *wise* up. It would never have worked; the pair of you would have been in the divorce courts within a year if Chris had ever been fool enough to take you up on what you're so pathetically desperate to give him.'

'You don't *know* that,' Poppy had spat back angrily. '*You* don't anything.'

'Oh, no,' James had mocked her softly. 'You don't know *what* I know.' He had added, 'And if you did…' He had paused, smiling nastily at her before challenging her with, 'Of course, if you ever feel like finding out…'

'I hate you, James,' Poppy had retaliated passionately.

No, she would never marry now, and all Sally's determined attempt to engineer it so that she was one of the trio to catch the bridal bouquet had done was reinforce that fact.

CHAPTER ONE

SLOWLY, gravely, Poppy knelt in front of the bonfire that she had just constructed, oblivious to the damp seeping into the knees of her jeans, the dying rays of the evening sunlight turning her silky brown hair a dark, rich red and illuminating her in a beam of light as, head bowed, she carefully struck a match with such seriousness that she might have been igniting a funeral pyre.

Which in effect she was, Poppy acknowledged tiredly as she watched the kindling that she had carefully arranged start to burn, flames crackling as they ran from twig to twig, racing towards the wooden trinket box at their heart.

As she stood up Poppy had to dig her hands deep into the pockets of her jeans to prevent herself pulling the kindling aside and snatching the box to safety.

It was over, she told herself mercilessly, closing her eyes, unable to look, unable to watch almost a whole decade of ceaseless devotion and love being eaten up by flames. A sharp breeze sprang up out of nowhere, ruffling the silky curtain of her hair, scattering sparks from the fire, whirling-dervish-like, amongst its flames, teasing them, snatching from them a handful of photographs, most of them charred beyond recognition, only one of them still recognisable, the pale pink lipstick shape of her own mouth imprinted brightly across its surface.

Tears stung Poppy's eyes, her heart twisting and aching with anguish as her emotions overcame her will-power and she stretched out helplessly to clasp the photograph which fate, it seemed, had decreed that she should not destroy.

As Chris's beloved features swam before her, tears filled her eyes and she missed the photograph, the wind whirling it out of reach. With a small cry, Poppy tried to pursue it, but someone else reached it before her, taking it from the breeze's playful grasp with mocking ease, a taunting expression crossing his saturnine face as he looked at it and then back at her.

'James!' Poppy said his name with loathing as he came down the garden towards her, still holding her photograph.

James might be her beloved, darling Chris's elder brother and her cousin but no two men could have been more unalike, Poppy reflected bitterly as James stopped walking and studied her bonfire.

Whereas Chris was all sunny smiles, warmth and laughter, good natured, easygoing, an open, uncomplicated individual whom it had all been too heartbreakingly easy for her to fall in love with, James was just the opposite.

James rarely smiled, or at least not at her, and James was most certainly not good-natured, nor easygoing and certainly not uncomplicated; even those who liked and approved of him, such as her mother, were forced to admit that he was not always the easiest person in the world to deal with.

'It's because he had to step into his father's shoes whilst he was still so young,' her mother always said in his defence.

'He was only twenty when Howard died, after all, and he had to take full responsibility for looking after his mother and Chris, as well as the business.'

Her mother had to defend James because he was her nephew. Poppy knew that but she hated him, loathed him, and she knew that he reciprocated those feelings even if he cloaked his in a more urbane and taunting mockery towards her than she could ever achieve towards him. It shocked her that people who didn't really know them always claimed that of the two brothers James was by far the better looking...

'He's very, very dangerously sexy,' one of the girls who worked for the small family company which James had taken over on his father's death had told her.

According to her mother, by hard work and dedication he had built the company into something far more impressive than it had ever been during his father's day.

'I'll just bet he's a real once-in-a-lifetime experience in bed,' the girl had added forthrightly.

Poppy had shuddered to listen to her, thinking that if she *really* knew what James was like, how cruel and hard he could be, she wouldn't think that. Personally Poppy couldn't think of any man she'd want less as a lover, but then there was only one man that Poppy wanted to fulfil that role in her life...in her heart...in her bed, and there always had been.

She had been twelve years old, a girl just on the brink of womanhood, when she had looked across the table at her first semi-grown-up birthday party and fallen head over heels in love with Chris. And she had gone on loving him and hoping, praying, longing for him to love her in return, not just as his cousin but as a woman . . . *the* woman. Only he hadn't done so.

Instead he had fallen in love with someone else. Instead he had fallen in love with pretty, funny Sally. Sally, who was now his wife . . . Sally, whom Poppy couldn't hate even though she had tried very hard to do so.

Chris and James didn't even look very much like brothers, if you discounted the fact that they shared the same impressive height and breadth of shoulder, Poppy decided now, watching James in angry resentment. Whereas Chris had the warm good looks of a young sun-god, his floppy brown hair golden at the ends, his eyes the same blue as a warm summer sky, his skin a mouth-watering gold, James looked more demoniac than godlike . . .

Like Chris, he too had inherited his Italian grandmother's warm skin colouring, but in James it was somehow harder, more aggressively masculine, bronzer than Chris's softer gold, just as his eyes were a far harder and colder nerve-freezing light aqua— the kind of eyes that could chill your blood to ice from three metres away if they chose. His hair, too, was much darker than Chris's—not black but certainly very dark brown, with dark flecks of burnt gold that gleamed like amber in the sunlight.

Poppy was not a complete fool; she could see that physically some women might be drawn to a man of James's type, and that of his type, perhaps, as the girl at work had said, he was an outstanding example, but *she* could never find him attractive. There was his temper, an ice-cold, rapier-sharp, humiliatingly effective weapon of destruction onto which she had run in furious, blind hotheadedness more times than she could bear to remember, and his sarcasm, which could rip your pride to shreds like the mountain cougar's velvet-sheathed claws.

'What the hell is going on?' he demanded now as he walked towards her.

Mutinously Poppy glowered at him. He hadn't looked at the photograph as yet and she itched to demand its return, her stomach muscles cramping with tension.

'Mum and Dad are out,' she told him ungraciously. 'There's only me here...'

'It's you I wanted to see,' James told her urbanely, walking past her to squat down on his heels and study her bonfire.

Why was it, Poppy thought, watching warily, that such an action by any other man dressed as James was now—in an expensive, immaculately tailored business suit, highly polished shoes and a pristine white shirt—would have immediately rendered him ridiculous, but made James look completely the opposite? And why, she demanded irritably of life, should the bonfire—*her* bonfire—deposit its unwanted windborne detritus of smoke and sooty smudges in her direction and not his?

Life just wasn't fair...

Fresh tears smarted in her eyes. Hastily she blinked them away just as she heard James commenting sardonically, 'What exactly is the purpose of all this self-sacrifice Poppy? Not, one trusts, some immature and ignoble hope that out of the ashes of this maudlin act a new and stronger love for Chris will rise, like a phoenix, only this time one that he shares, because if so—'

'Of course not,' Poppy denied swiftly, too shocked by his contemptuous accusation to pretend not to understand what he meant—or to deny the purpose of the bonfire.

It was typical, of course; only James could make that kind of assumption about her motivation for doing something; only James would accuse her so unfairly.

'If you must know,' she told him bitterly, 'I was trying to do what you've been telling me I should do for years, and that is to accept that Chris doesn't . . . that he never—' She broke off, swallowing hard as her emotions threatened to overwhelm her.

'Damn you to hell, James,' she swore shakily. 'This has nothing to do with you . . . and you have no right—'

'I *am* Chris's brother,' he reminded her crisply, 'and as such it's my brotherly duty to protect him and his marriage from—'

'From what?' Poppy demanded shakily. 'From *me* . . .?' Bitterly she started to laugh. 'From me,' she repeated. 'From my love—'

'Your *love*!' James interrupted her, his mouth twisting. 'You don't even begin to know the meaning of the word. In the eyes of the world you might be a mature woman of twenty-two, but inside you're still an adolescent,' he told her crushingly, 'with all the danger to yourself and to others that that implies.'

'I am not an adolescent,' Poppy denied furiously, angry flags of temper burning in her cheeks.

'The way you can't control your emotions says that you are,' James corrected her coldly. 'And, like an adolescent,' he continued bitingly, 'you positively enjoy wallowing in your self-induced misery, the selfaggrandised "love" you claim you feel for Chris. But you, of course, being you, have to drag everyone else into the plot as well.'

'That's not true,' Poppy gasped furiously. 'You—'

'It is true,' James told her grimly. 'Look at the way you behaved at the wedding ... Do you think that a single person there didn't know what you were doing, or how you felt?'

'I wasn't *do*ing anything,' Poppy protested, her face as white now as it had been red before.

'Yes, you were,' James told her. 'You were trying to make Chris feel guilty and to make everyone else feel sorry for you. Well, it isn't people's pity you deserve, Poppy...it's their contempt. If you really loved Chris—*really* loved him—you'd put his happiness before your own selfish, self-induced misery.

'You claim that you're not an adolescent any longer, that you're an adult. Well, try behaving like one,' James told her witheringly.

'You have no right to speak to me like that,' Poppy told him chokingly. 'You have no idea how I feel or what—'

She froze as James burst out laughing—a harsh, contemptuous sound that splintered the early evening air.

'No idea...? My dear Poppy, the whole town knows how *you* feel.'

Poppy stared at him.

'Nothing to say?' he jeered.

Poppy swallowed painfully. People did know how she felt about Chris. She couldn't deny that, but not because she had deliberately flaunted her feelings to make Chris feel guilty, as James had so unfairly claimed.

It was simply that she had been so young when she had first fallen in love with Chris that it had been impossible for her to keep her feelings hidden, and she had loved him so long that people were bound to have noticed. But she had never, ever, as James was claiming, used her feelings to try to manipulate Chris, or, indeed, anyone else, into feeling sorry for her.

Of course, she deplored the fact that people *were* aware of her love for Chris—why else on the evening when he and Sally had broken the news of their engagement to the family had she made a silent vow that somehow she had to find a way to stop loving him?

All right, so far she might not have been successful, but at least she had tried—and was still trying.

It should have helped, she knew, knowing that Sally was so right for Chris and that they were so very, very much in love; with any other girl but Sally she might have suspected that that gesture of hers in ensuring that Poppy was one of the trio who was tricked into catching Sally's wedding bouquet had been, at best, a clear warning to her that it was time for her to find a man of her own and, at worst, a tauntingly vindictive underlining of the fact that she had lost Chris. But Sally was far too genuinely nice and warm-hearted to do anything like that and her motives, Poppy knew, had been completely altruistic.

That hadn't stopped it hurting, though. And now here was James deliberately making that hurting worse.

'How I feel ... what I do is none of your business,' was the only response she could manage to James's taunt.

'No?' James gave her an ironic look. 'Well, what *is* my business is the fact that you are employed by the company as a linguist and interpreter and, as such, I see that you're down to fly out to Italy for the international conference next Wednesday.'

'Yes,' Poppy agreed listlessly. The previous year, when the conference had been arranged, she had believed that Chris would be representing the company at the conference, and when he had asked her if she would like to go too she had walked on air for days afterwards, her imagination fuelling wildly romantic and, she realised, looking back, totally impossible fantasies featuring the two of them.

The reality, she knew now, would be rather different. Even if Chris had still been going, the four days of the conference would be filled with meetings, whilst she would be called upon to use her language skills, both in verbal translations and paperwork, which from previous experience she knew would keep her tied to her hotel bedroom when she wasn't actually attending the conference with the company's small sales team.

'The flight time's been changed,' James informed her. 'I'll pick you up here at six-thirty. I've got to drive past on my way to the airport, so—'

'*You'll* pick me up?' Poppy interrupted him, shocked. 'But you aren't going. Chris...'

'*Chris* is on honeymoon, as you very well know, and won't be back for another week,' James reminded her grimly, giving her a tauntingly sardonic look as he added unkindly, 'Surely even you aren't self-deluding enough to believe that he'd cut short his honeymoon to go to Italy with you? Or was that what you were secretly hoping, Poppy... secretly wishing he would do? My God, just when the hell are you going to grow up and realise that—'

'That what?' Poppy interrupted him furiously, fighting to control the way her mouth had started to tremble as she goaded James wildly. 'Go on, then, say it. Say what we both know you're just dying to say, James. Or shall I say it for you...?'

Her chin tilted proudly as she forced herself to look straight into his eyes without flinching. 'When am I going to realise that Chris doesn't love me, that he will never love me... that he loves Sally...?' she said bravely.

She knew that her eyes were over-bright with betraying tears, but she couldn't help it; her emotions were too strong for her, too overpowering.

'Of course I know that Chris won't be going to Italy,' she told James tiredly, turning away from him as the box at the heart of her small bonfire suddenly crackled fiercely and was engulfed by flames.

The pain inside her heart as she watched it burn was so sharp and driving that she had to force herself not to reach into the fire and retrieve the box, shaking it from the flames. Inside it were all her precious, cherished memories and souvenirs of her years of loving Chris: the present he had given her for that momentous twelfth birthday when she had first fallen in love with him... the card he had sent her... the other gifts he had given her over the years.

Quite mundane, perhaps, in many ways, and certainly not the gifts of a lover; no doubt in James, for instance, the small, precious hoard that she had guarded so tenderly would only provoke derision and contempt, but to her...

Yes, she had known that Chris wouldn't be going to Italy, but it had never occurred to her that James would be attending the conference in his place. She had assumed that someone else from the sales team would go instead. She frowned suddenly, something striking her.

'If you're going to Italy, you won't need me there,' she announced as she turned back to look at him. 'You speak Italian fluently.'

As well he might, Poppy reflected ungenerously. After all, his grandmother on his mother's side was Italian and both he and Chris had frequently spent summer holidays with their Italian relations. But whereas James had always been very fluent in the language, Chris had not absorbed it quite so well.

'Italian, yes,' James agreed coolly, 'but this is an international conference, remember, and your knowledge of Japanese is required. So, if you were entertaining any ideas about spending your time mooning around daydreaming about Chris, I warn you that we're going to Italy to work...'

'You don't have any right to warn *me* about anything,' Poppy challenged him dangerously, inwardly seething with resentment at the fact that he had called her professionalism into question.

She was well aware how strenuously he had opposed her appointment to the post of interpreter and translator within the company, sneering that it was nepotism and that it would be cheaper to send such work out to tender.

She shouldn't have been listening outside the office door when he and her mother had argued about her appointment, Poppy knew, and she really hadn't intended to do so but had simply been on her way to see her mother.

However, what she had heard him say about her had made her all the more determined to prove just how wrong he was and just how valuable she could be to the company, and she had immediately put aside her own initial doubts about the wisdom of going to work for the family electronics business.

When her mother had first suggested that she did so, Poppy had been reluctant to agree, wanting instead to establish her independence, but the knowledge of how difficult it was proving for her to find a job by herself, coupled with the fact that she'd known she would be working closely with Chris, had overcome her scruples and she now firmly believed that in the short time she had been with the company she had proved her worth.

'I *know* I'm going to Italy to work,' Poppy added pointedly now. 'After all, I'm not the one who...'

She paused, alarmed by the look in James's eyes which told her that she had gone too far.

'Go on,' he invited silkily, his voice suddenly softly dangerous.

'Well, I'm not the one with the family in Italy,' Poppy blustered, shrugging.

'Are you trying to say that I'm using the company to finance my own personal plans?' James suggested ominously.

'Well, you aren't exactly involved in the sales side of things, are you?' Poppy demanded aggressively. 'The sales team—'

'As managing director and chairman of the company, I am involved in everything,' James told her softly. 'Everything... Not so much as a paper-clip disappears without my knowing about it, Poppy, you may be sure of that,' he told her with a wintry look that made her colour up hotly as she remembered the occasions on which she had 'borrowed' company stationery.

'And as for the sales team... On this occasion,' he told her smoothly, 'they won't be coming with us.'

'With *us*?' Poppy stared at him in disbelief. 'You mean it will be just you and me...?' She couldn't keep the horror out of her voice.

'Just you and me,' James confirmed.

'I'm not... I won't...' Poppy began, and then stopped as James suddenly smiled at her gently...too gently, her instincts warned her as she wondered edgily if refusing to accompany him would be grounds for dismissal from her job. James was clever like that...sneaky enough too, and she knew how much he had always resented the fact that she was working for the company.

'You're the boss,' she told him, attempting a careless shrug but suspecting from the narrow-eyed, glinting look of mockery that he was giving her that she hadn't really deceived him.

Four days in Italy with James... She tried not to shudder. She couldn't think of anything that came closer to her idea of purgatory.

She winced as a cloud of acrid smoke from her bonfire was suddenly blown into her face, making her cough and choke. As she stumbled clear of it, she saw that James was studying the photograph that he had snatched from the wind, and she could feel the hot tide of embarrassed colour starting to burn her face.

It was not the fact that the photograph was of Chris that bothered her; it was an old one taken when she had been fourteen and he seventeen. She had taken it herself, snatching it with her new camera at a family party, and had later, with great daring, had the original print blown up.

No, what was causing her whole body to burn with humiliated embarrassment was the fact that virtually the whole of Chris's face, but most especially his mouth, was covered in tell-tale lipstick kisses where she had deliberately—oh, shaming to remember now—pressed her open lips with passionate intensity against Chris's.

A wave of toe-curling, excruciatingly horrible embarrassment, more intense than any self-consciousness she had ever suffered before, poured through her with scalding heat. Her body tensed in readiness for James's taunting laughter as she resisted the desire to compound her humiliation by reaching out to try to snatch the betraying photograph from him.

But, instead of laughing, James was simply looking from the photograph to her . . . to her mouth, she recognised with searing misery...and then back again...

Unable to bear the nerve-stretching silence of James's clinical study of her any longer, Poppy gave in to temptation and did what she had promised herself she was now mature enough not to do—she darted quickly towards him, reaching out her hand to snatch the photograph from him. But as she reached him he realised what she was trying to do and grabbed hold of her with one hand, whilst retaining possession of her photograph with the other.

'Let me go,' Poppy demanded, all sense of restraint and dignity overwhelmed by the humiliation-fuelled anger that gripped her, her hands pummelling furiously against James's chest as she writhed impotently against him, struggling to break free.

She had no chance of doing so, of course; her brain knew that even if her emotions and her body refused to accept it.

James was a good six feet two to her five-four and at least five stone heavier; add to that the fact that she knew perfectly well that he swam and ran regularly as well as practising the art of aikido and it was no wonder that her furious attempts to break free were doing more to exhaust her strength than his.

Even so, she still persisted, demanding through gritted teeth, 'Let go of me ... James ... and give me back my photograph ...'

'Your photograph.' Now he did laugh—a harsh, contemptuous sound that made her long to clap her hands over her ears to protect herself. 'I suppose this is the nearest you've ever come to kissing a man with passion, isn't it, Poppy? After all—'

'No, of course it isn't,' Poppy denied untruthfully. She was damned if she was going to let James make her feel even worse than she already did.

'No?' James queried silkily, his eyes narrowing cynically as Poppy inadvertently looked up at him. 'So who was he, then? It certainly wasn't Chris, and yet, according to you, he's the only man you've ever loved ... the only man you could ever love ...'

Poppy's face flushed scarlet with fury as she realised that James was quoting back at her the impassioned words that her sixteen-year-old self had declared to him when he had asked her tauntingly if she had grown out of her crush on his younger brother yet.

'No one you know,' Poppy shot back at him furiously. 'In fact...'

'No one anyone knows, including you, is more like it,' James contradicted her drily.

'That's not true,' Poppy lied hotly.

'No?' James taunted her. 'Well, let's just put it to the test, shall we...?'

Before she knew what he intended to do, somehow he had shifted his weight and hers, so that she was momentarily off balance and forced instinctively to reach out and cling to him for support, whilst he took advantage of her vulnerability to tighten his hold on her, using not just one but both arms this time to imprison her against him, holding her so close that she could actually feel the hard, firmly muscled length of his thigh against her and the equally firm thud of his heart.

'James,' she began, automatically tilting her head back so that she could look at him and show him how angry she was, but her complaint died away in her throat as she saw the way he was looking at her... at her mouth... and her own heart began to trip frantically in a series of far too fast, shallow little beats that made her breathing quicken and her muscles tense, her lips parting as she tried to draw extra air into her suddenly oxygen-deprived lungs.

A small sound—a protest, a soft moan; even she wasn't quite sure which—gasped its way past the locked muscles of her throat and was lost, stifled by the slow, deliberate pressure of James's mouth against hers.

This couldn't be happening, Poppy thought, her mind reeling with shock and disbelief. James's mouth against hers, covering it, caressing it, possessing it...

Frantically, she tried to turn her head out of the way, panic flooding her body with a trembling agitation and a desperate need to break free, but James forestalled her, one hand still binding her firmly against his body whilst the other grasped a handful of her hair, twisting it through his fingers, and then cupped her jaw, imprisoning her beneath the growing pressure of a kiss that was making her feel increasingly vulnerable.

She could feel the strength in his fingers where they rested against her skin, their touch cool in marked contrast to the burning heat of her own flushed face, just as the steady thud of his heartbeat underlined the wretchedly fast race of her own.

She knew, shamingly, that she was trembling from head to foot, and she knew, even more humiliatingly, that James must know it too. She could feel his fingers sliding along her throat, stroking her skin gently... *gently* ... James.

Tears blurred her vision, burning behind the eyelids she refused to close as she glared her enmity into the cool, clear aqua of James's unreadable eyes.

All these years of dreaming of Chris kissing her, Chris holding her, Chris's mouth caressing and possessing hers, and now it had to be *James* who was turning what should have been one of the most treasured moments of her life into a mocking parody of everything that her first kiss of real passion should have been.

Was it really for this that she had refused dates and explorative teenage snogging sessions? Was it for this that she had held aloof from the sexual freedom that university could have afforded her? Was it for this that she had spent her nights and some of her days

dreaming and yearning...? So that James could mock
her and destroy her cherished fantasies with a cruel
kiss that could only be designed to taunt her—a kiss
that...?

Poppy stiffened as her brain belatedly recognised
something that her traitorous senses had shamingly
already seemed to acknowledge—namely that if it
hadn't actually been James, her loathed elder cousin,
whose mouth was caressing hers she might
almost...could almost...

Poppy gave an outraged gasp as she realised just
why her lips, her mouth, seemed to be softening,
yielding, almost enjoying the sensual contact with
James's, her eyes snapping fire when she registered
the sudden, heart-stopping gleam darkening James's
as he finally lifted his mouth from hers.

Her legs felt oddly weak as she stepped back from
him, Poppy recognised dizzily—and not just her legs
either.

'Well, whoever he was, if indeed he did actually
exist,' she heard James saying derisively to her, 'he
wasn't a very good teacher. Either that or...'

'Or what?' Poppy recovered just enough to challenge him. 'I wasn't a very good pupil...?'

'Oh, I wouldn't say that.'

Poppy stared at him, caught between disbelief and
suspicion, waiting for the taunting barb that she was
sure was to come, but instead he simply stood there
whilst her gaze dropped helplessly from his eyes to
his mouth—in fact it might have been jerked there on
strings which he controlled, so little ability did she
have to stop its betraying movement.

'Yes?' she heard James murmur invitingly.

'Give me back my photograph,' Poppy demanded huskily, determinedly forcing her gaze back to his eyes, hoping that he would put the hot colour burning her face down to the heat of her bonfire.

But, instead of acceding to her demand, to her disbelief James tore the photograph—*her* precious photograph—into small pieces and then casually walked over to the now dying bonfire and dropped them into its burning embers.

'You had no right to do that,' Poppy protested chokily. 'That...'

'What else did you intend to do with it?' James asked her. 'It's over, Poppy. Chris is married now. Accept it; he never loved you and he never will,' he told her cruelly.

'How dare you—' she began.

But he stopped her, continuing bluntly, 'And it's time you grew up and accepted the truth instead of living in an adolescent fantasy world.'

He had started to walk away from her, to Poppy's relief. Seeing him tear up her precious photograph and consign it to the bonfire had brought back all her earlier misery and despair and she knew that tears weren't very far away. She had humiliated herself enough without James seeing her cry.

He paused and she tensed as he turned round to look at her.

'Don't forget,' he warned her, 'I'll pick you up at six-thirty on Wednesday morning. Don't be late...'

CHAPTER TWO

POPPY woke up abruptly and stared anxiously at the illuminated face of her alarm clock, her heart thumping in dread at the thought that she might have overslept.

Five o'clock. She let her breath out in a sigh of relief and switched off the alarm, which she had set for five-thirty, as she swung her legs out of her bed. She hadn't slept well at all—and not just last night, but every night since the wedding, and, if she was honest with herself, for a long time before that too.

Yesterday she had come home to find her mother and her aunt poring over the proofs of the wedding photographs.

It had hurt her to see the way both of them had looked slightly uncomfortable at her arrival. It had been exactly the same at the wedding, she acknowledged: people treating her with the kind of well-intentioned caution and sympathy which was meant to be compassionate but which had the effect of somehow making her feel just the opposite. An outsider . . . a spectre at the feast.

The only person who had treated her anything like normally had been the other bridesmaid—and Sally's oldest and closest friend—who Poppy had quickly learned held a very cynical and wryly funny view of relationships and commitment.

'Love may not last, but, believe me, enmity does,' Star had told Poppy grimly during one of their bridesmaid-dress fittings, 'and I've got the parents to prove it. I swear that mine pour more energy and emotion into loathing one another and fighting with one another than they ever did into their marriage, their supposed love.'

She had seen the way her aunt had surreptitiously slid out of sight the photographs of the bride and groom in happy, loving close-ups as they kissed for the camera, and as she'd walked out of the kitchen she had heard her aunt telling her mother how much she liked Sally, and how very, very much in love with her Chris was.

'I never thought he would fall so deeply in love,' Poppy heard her adding as she paused on the stairs, not wanting to listen and yet somehow unable to stop herself. She was a masochist addicted to the source of her pain, she told herself bitterly as the older woman continued.

'Of the two of them James has always been the more passionate and intense one. Chris has always had a much sunnier, more resilient nature. I just wish... How is Poppy? She...'

Quickly Poppy moved out of earshot, her body trembling inwardly with a mixture of pain and indignation.

She knew how James would have reacted if he had been privy to that conversation, how he would have taunted her for allowing herself to become the object of other people's pity—something *he* would never allow to happen to him. Poppy's mouth twisted into a small, bitter smile as she tried to imagine James being involved in any situation, any relationship which might cast him in such a role. Impossible.

It was all very well for her aunt to describe James as the more intense of her two sons—maybe he was, Poppy allowed, though she thought it more a case of his being intent on having his own way and steam-rollering anyone who stood in opposition to him. But more passionate? And because of that passion, as her aunt had somehow implied, more vulnerable than his more easygoing younger brother? No way.

The only intense passion she had ever seen James exhibit was that of anger—the kind of anger that she had felt when he had given her that unwanted, hateful kiss of contempt.

Poppy shivered now as she hurried into the bathroom, the chill invading her body—that tiny, be-traying sensation—nothing at all to do with the coolness of the early morning air.

In fact, as she glanced through the window she could see that the pre-dawn sky was clear and that it promised to be a fine, warm day.

No, the reason for the almost electric shock of sen-sitivity raising goose bumps on her skin lay not outside her body but within it. Its cause was her own fiercely denied and totally shocked awareness of the fact that something within her, some alien, unknown, un-wanted part of her, had been physically responsive to the practised skill of James's kiss.

It wasn't a subject that she had any desire to ex-plore and in order to dismiss it she spent her brief time under the shower running through the list of Japanese technical terms that she had committed to memory the previous evening.

The conference they were attending was a new one and it promised to be a highly prestigious event. Until James had announced that he would be going, taking the place not just of Chris but also of the sales team, Poppy had been looking forward to it.

The venue was not Milan, where she had been on previous occasions, but a newly opened, exclusive spa resort in the mountains, and the brochure that Chris had shown her had made the event read more like an exclusive holiday than a work event.

Not that she would have any time to enjoy the facilities of the spa, Poppy reflected as she stepped out of the shower and reached for a towel. James, she suspected, would see to that.

As she reached for her underclothes she caught sight of her naked body in the bathroom mirror. She had always been slim but during the weeks leading up to the wedding she had lost weight and now, she acknowledged, she was getting close to looking almost thin. Mentally comparing her fragile, slender body with Sally's almost voluptuously feminine shape, she admitted that it was no wonder that Chris should prefer the open sensuality of Sally's body to the fine-boned thinness of hers.

James had commented derisively on her lack of feminine curves only the previous Christmas, when they'd had their obligatory dance together at the firm's Christmas party. His hands had spanned her waist completely and he'd taunted her with the fact that her body was more that of a girl than of a woman.

'Just another indication of your reluctance to grow up and accept life as it really is,' had been his sardonic comment.

'I am adult; I'm twenty-two years old,' Poppy had countered angrily.

'On the outside,' James had agreed, 'but inside you're still an adolescent clinging to a self-created fantasy. You don't have an inkling of what real life is all about, Poppy...real emotions...real men.'

She had denied his comments, of course, but it hadn't made any difference.

It hadn't always been like this between them; they hadn't always shared an enmity which seemed to deepen and harden with the years instead of relaxing and easing.

As a child she had adored James. *He* had then been the one who had rescued her from *Chris's* teasing, the one who had patiently taught her to ride her first bike, fly her first kite, the one who had mopped up her tears when she'd fallen off the former and over the strings of the latter.

But all that had changed when she was twelve and had fallen in love with Chris. James's good-humoured, elder-cousin indulgence of her had turned to contemptuous hostility once he had recognised her feelings for Chris, and she had reciprocated with a fury and dislike which had grown over the years instead of abating.

The last thing she wanted to do, she admitted to herself as she dressed quickly in her working 'uniform' of cream silk shirt and straight skirt of her taupe suit, was to spend the next four days exposed to James's contempt and hostility, but it was not in her nature to take the cowardly way out of refusing to go; she took her job too seriously for that.

The actual translation work she did might not be enough to keep her busy eight hours a day, five days a week, Poppy acknowledged, but a look around at the kind of job her peers had been forced to take—some of them with much better degrees than her own—had made her determined to prove her worth to the business; an evening course in computer technology had turned out to be a wise investment of her time, as had her determination to involve herself in the administrative side of the business.

To some, such work might have seemed mundane, but Poppy felt it had given her a working knowledge and an insight into the running of the company which would be just as valuable on any future CV she needed to prepare as her language skills and her degree.

The overnight bag which she had packed the night before was downstairs in the hall. Picking up her suit jacket she studied her reflection in her bedroom mirror critically.

Her hair, soft and straight, made her look younger than she actually was, she knew, but she was loath to have it cut. Chris had once told her that he thought long hair on a woman was incredibly feminine. Sally, though, oddly enough, had a short, almost boyish crop of blonde curls.

Her features didn't lend themselves well to exaggerated make-up and her skin was too pale, she decided critically. Her eyes, her best feature, were large and almond-shaped and fringed with thick dark lashes which looked ridiculous when loaded down with mascara. Her nose was short and straight, and her mouth, in her view, was an odd mismatch, her top lip well shaped and moderately curved whilst her bottom lip was wider and fuller, somehow giving her mouth a sensuality which she personally found distressing and which she always tried to play down with a softly coloured matt lipstick.

So far the early spring weather had been unseasonably fine and warm and her skin had begun to lose its winter pallor, but she had still slipped on stockings beneath her skirt. Bare legs, no matter how blissfully cool, did not, in her opinion, look properly businesslike.

Downstairs she made herself a cup of coffee and a slice of toast which she knew she wouldn't eat. Her stomach was already churning nervously. She had never particularly liked flying.

James and Chris's father, her uncle, had been a keen amateur pilot who had been killed with a friend when they had flown into a freak electric storm. She remembered how devastated Chris had been at his father's death. They had cried over it together, sharing their grief. James, on the other hand, had retreated into grim, white-faced silence—a remote stranger, or so it had seemed to Poppy, who'd looked contemptuously upon her and Chris's shared emotional grief.

She heard James's car just as she was swallowing her last mouthful of coffee. Quickly putting down her cup she hurried out into the hall, pulling on her jacket and picking up her handbag and case as she went to open the door. Like her, James was dressed formally in a business suit, not navy for once but a lightweight pale grey which somehow emphasised his height and the breadth of his shoulders.

As he took her case from her, Poppy saw the brief, assessing glance he gave her and her chin started to tilt challengingly as she waited for him to make some critical or derogatory comment, but instead, disconcertingly, she suddenly became aware that his original scrutiny had turned into something a little more thorough and startlingly more male as his eyes lingered on the soft curves of her breasts.

It was the kind of inspection that Poppy was used to from other men; that telling but, generally speaking, acceptably discreet male awareness of her as a woman. But to be subjected to it by *James* ... James who'd sternly reprimanded his younger brother when Chris had teasingly commented on her new shape the first day she had self-consciously worn the pretty, flower-sprigged cotton bra that her mother had gravely agreed that her eleven-year-old's barely thirty-inch chest demanded.

Seeing James focus on that same chest in such a very male and sensual way when for years Poppy could have sworn that he was totally oblivious to the fact that she had grown from a child to a woman was a very disconcerting experience.

Somehow just managing to resist the temptation to tug the edges of her jacket protectively together, Poppy gave him an angry glare. How would he like it if she focused on ... a certain part of his body in that way.

'Have you got everything?' she heard him ask her before her brain could come up with an answer to her own question. 'Tickets, passport, money...?'

'Of course,' Poppy responded, grittily withholding the angry comment she wanted to make. This was a business trip to Italy, she reminded herself grimly, and she intended to preserve a businesslike distance between them, if only to prove to James that she was not the adolescent child he constantly taunted her as being.

Outside, his Jaguar gleamed richly in the early morning sunshine. As he opened the passenger door for her, Poppy could smell the rich, expensive scent of the car's leather seats. Chris and her mother, who, like James, were directors and shareholders in the company, drove cars with far less status and the urge to remind James of this fact was irresistible as he slid into the driver's seat next to her and started the car.

'Very nice,' she commented, smoothing the cream leather with her fingertips. 'A perk of the job, I presume...?'

'No, as a matter of fact, it isn't,' James shocked her by denying as he swung the car into the traffic. 'It's time you brought yourself up to date with current tax laws, Poppy,' he told her acidly. 'Even if I wanted to make use of my...connection with the company to my own financial advantage, the current tax penalties involved in owning an expensive company car would prohibit me from doing so.'

Poppy could feel her face start to burn as she interpreted the message in the first part of his statement. Unlike her, *he* did not have to benefit from his connection with the company, he was implying.

Resentment burned angrily in Poppy's chest. Was she *never* going to be judged on her own merits, instead of being condemned because of her mother's position as a shareholder? How would James like it if she pointed out to him that the only reason he was the company's chairman was because of his father?

Poppy moved irritably against the restriction of her seat belt, all too aware of how easily James could refute such an accusation. Although he had the reputation within the company of being a demanding employer, noone disputed the fact that the company's present success was due to his hard work. And no matter how much he might demand of those who worked for him it was never any more than he demanded of himself.

The traffic was starting to build up as they got closer to the airport and already Poppy's stomach was be-

ginning to clench nervously as she anticipated what
lay ahead. It was the moment of take-off she dreaded
most; once that was over it was easier for her to relax.

The spot in Italy where the conference was being
held was three hours' drive from the airport, which
meant, Poppy suspected, that they would be spending
the better part of the day travelling. She had brought
some work with her to keep her occupied during the
flight—and to ensure that she didn't have to talk to
James—but she couldn't help wistfully reflecting how
different things would have been if her travelling
companion had been Chris...a Chris who was not
married to Sally or anyone else, a Chris who—

Stop it, she warned herself sternly. He *is* married
to Sally and you've got to stop thinking about
him...stop loving him...

As she quickly blinked away the weak tears she
could feel threatening her, she heard James say sardonically, 'Poor Poppy, still hopelessly in love with a
man who doesn't want her. Why do I get the impression it's a role you actively enjoy playing?' he
asked her savagely, the harshness in his voice shocking
her almost as much as the cruelty of his accusation.

'That's not true,' she denied chokily.

'That's not the impression I get,' James said to her
as he negotiated the maze of slip-roads that led to the
car park. 'In fact I'd say the role of self-pitying lover
is one you've embraced with far more enthusiasm than
you appear to have had for embracing *real* love.'

Poppy's face burned hotly as he parked the car and
opened his door. She wasn't going to dignify his comments by responding to them...or defending herself,
she told herself fiercely. Nor was she going to let James
see how much they had hurt her.

'It's no wonder that Chris prefers to take a real woman to bed,' James told her cruelly as he opened her door for her and waited like a gaoler for her to get out.

I *am* a real woman, Poppy wanted to protest. Just as real as Sally, just as capable of giving love, of inciting passion and desire. But was she? Was there something inherently feminine and desirable in Sally that was missing from her? Was she somehow lacking in that vital ingredient that made a woman lovable and desirable?

All the doubts about herself and her sexuality which had sprung into life with the news of Chris's engagement to Sally and which she had rigorously and fiercely ignored and denied suddenly rose up inside her, a fully armed enemy force which James's words had carelessly set free from the prison in which she had concealed them.

Did he know about the fears, the insecurities about her sexuality that these last months had brought? Poppy wondered numbly as she waited for him to remove their cases from the boot of his car.

How could he? It was impossible. He was simply trying to goad her, to hurt her, to provoke a reaction from her which would enable him to reinforce his condemnation of her as immature and foolish.

Quite what his purpose was in doing this Poppy didn't really know, had never really questioned. The enmity which had developed between them had grown alongside her love for Chris until she'd accepted it in the same way that she had accepted that love. But, despite the fact that Chris's marriage had now forced her to accept that she had to find a way of severing herself from the past and finding another focus for her life, of accepting that Chris could never be a part of that life in the way she had so much hoped, it seemed that since the wedding James's antagonism to her had simply increased.

Why? Was he perhaps trying to force her into leaving the company? Was his desire to hurt her, to undermine her... to destroy her... to do with the business, or something more personal?

James had locked the car and was waiting impatiently for her to join him.

These next four days were going to be the longest of her life, Poppy reflected.

'You can relax now; we're airborne...'

The sound of James's voice in her ear made Poppy open her tightly closed eyes, her pent-up breath leaking in a relieved sigh from her lungs as she recognised the truth of what he was saying.

Having shudderingly refused the window-seat that James had offered her, she had fastened her seat belt and willed herself not to give in to her childhood need to have a familiar hand to cling to as the plane had taxied down the runway and started to lift off.

At least she had managed not to do that, although... Surreptitiously she slowly released the tense fingers she had not been able to stop herself from curling into the immaculate smoothness of James's suit jacket—and not just James's suit jacket, she acknowledged uncomfortably, but James's very solidly muscled arm as well.

His dry 'Thank you, Poppy' as she tried to remove her hand from his arm without him noticing what she had done made her flush guiltily and avoid looking at him.

Did he never feel afraid? she wondered bitterly. Did nothing ever dent that iron self-control of his? Had no one ever made him ache . . . hurt . . . yearn for her so much that nothing else . . . noone else mattered?

If anyone had, she had certainly never been aware of it, Poppy thought, but then she had been too involved in her own feelings to pay much attention to anyone else.

As always, now that they were actually airborne, her fear left her, her body starting to relax . . .

She refused the drink that the stewardess offered her and reached for her case and the work she had brought with her. James, she noticed, was already engrossed in some papers which he had removed from his briefcase. Well, at least whilst his attention was on them he wouldn't be able to pick on her, she decided with relief.

'Oh, James, just look at that view,' Poppy breathed, unable to keep the awed delight from her voice as she stared through their hire-car window at the panorama spread before them.

Transport had been arranged from the airport to the conference centre, but James had opted to make his own arrangements and independently hire a car, and Poppy had felt no trepidation at the thought of travelling with him, since she knew that not only was he a very safe driver but that he was also familiar with Italian roads.

The thought of spending three hours shut up in a car with only him for company had been a different matter and until they had started to climb into the mountains she had resolutely occupied herself with her own thoughts rather than try to engage him in any conversation. Conversations with James, she had decided bitterly, always seemed to lead to the same place—to them arguing.

Pride and her awareness of how unsympathetic and antagonistic towards her he was had prevented her from trying to defend herself by telling him that loving Chris had become a burden she desperately wanted to remove from her life.

Had they had a different relationship, had they been closer, had she felt able to trust him, to turn to him for help, she might have been able to admit to him how much she longed to have someone to confide in, someone to whom she could talk about her feelings and her guilt at her own inability to leave behind a love she knew could only cause her pain. If things had been different... if *he* had been different... if he had still been the same James he had been when she had been a child... But he wasn't, and somewhere, somehow, the cousinly love that he had once felt for her had gone.

Her determination not to give him any opportunity to criticise or condemn her whilst they were alone by keeping silent and aloof from him had disintegrated, though, as the road had started to wind through the ancient chain of mountains, taking them through small villages and dusty towns in whose Renaissance squares Poppy could very easily visualise the richly liveried men-at-arms who, along with the princes who had once commanded them, had fought over the prizes of the fertile plains below them.

Today, the towns were tranquil, only their architecture a reminder of the past turbulence and turmoil, the scenery around them so spectacular that it bewitched Poppy into forgetting her vow of silence to exclaim over its beauty.

James, of course, was bound to be less impressed, Poppy recognised; he had relatives in Tuscany and Rome and was no stranger to the beauty of Italy's countryside, nor her architecture. And Poppy told herself that she ought not to feel rather like a child told off for a crime it hadn't committed when James turned his head to look at her in response to her impulsive comment and said tautly, 'But no doubt a view which you would enjoy far more if it was my brother you were seeing it with. Too bad that Chris doesn't share your enthusiasm. He's a modern city man, Poppy—something else he and Sally share, something else you and he don't,' he told her unkindly.

Poppy said nothing, turning her head away so that James couldn't see the quick, betraying sheen of tears filming her eyes.

She knew, of course, that Chris did not share her love of history... of the past... of the awesomeness of nature, as James had just said, and as Chris himself was the first to cheerfully admit.

Nor did she intend to defend herself by contradicting James's comment or by telling him that he was wrong and that, oddly enough, she had not actually been wishing that Chris were in the car beside her.

She hadn't...but now she did, and with such heartaching intensity that she was almost swamped by her misery.

Thank heavens it couldn't be much further to the hotel, she thought. She closed her eyes and leaned back in her seat, keeping her face turned towards the window and averted from James.

Four days, four times twenty-four hours… She gave an involuntary shudder. Please God, let them pass quickly, she prayed.

'Poppy.'

Sleepily Poppy opened her eyes and eased her aching body into a more comfortable position when she realised that the car had come to a halt and that they had reached their destination.

The hotel, as she had read in the brochure, had originally been a medieval fortress built by an Italian prince, set high up in the mountains to guard his territories, but reading about it had not prepared her for the raw magnificence of a structure which seemed to be carved out of the rock itself, rising up steeply from the walled courtyard in which they were now parked.

Even though she knew that the original fortress was now just a shell which had been used to house a far more modern and luxurious centre, Poppy felt awe-struck and faintly intimidated by the sheer, stark rise of the stone edifice in front of her, which was softened only slightly by its mantle of ivy and roses.

The *palazzo* had been used as a private home for several centuries, abandoned only when it had been commandeered by the German army during the Second World War, and Poppy knew that in addition to the luxurious state rooms which had now been adapted to form the hotel's reception rooms the original Italian water garden had been restored to working order and restocked with the varieties of roses and other plants with which it would originally have been adorned.

And yet, despite knowing just how luxurious the spa promised to be and being hit by the heat of the sunshine when she stepped out of the car, unable to remove her gaze from the sheer sweep of rock from which the outer wall of the fortress had been cut, Poppy couldn't quite repress a small shiver.

'Not the kind of place you'd want to be incarcerated in as a prisoner,' she heard James saying behind her, his comment so exactly mirroring her own thoughts that she turned towards him in surprise as he added drily, 'I wouldn't give much for anyone's chance of escaping from here.'

'No.' Poppy agreed bleakly. A prisoner would probably have about as much chance of escaping from such a place as she had of escaping James over the next few days.

The car park was starting to fill up rapidly with other arrivals. Picking up their cases, James touched Poppy briefly on the shoulder.

'Reception seems to be that way. Let's go and get booked in before it develops into too much of a scrum.'

Once inside the hotel, the austere, almost forbidding impression of the fortress as a prison was totally banished by the breathtaking luxury of the reception area, a huge, vaulted room illuminated by crystal chandeliers, the walls decorated with glowingly rich frescos. Only a room this vast could take such an abundance of gold, crimson and blue, Poppy acknowledged dizzily as she followed James towards the central reception desk.

Immaculately groomed girls, in suits as understated as their surroundings were ornate, busied themselves dealing with the rapid influx of guests, and Poppy was cynically amused to see that James, who was in fact behind three other men trying to claim one girl's

attention, received the full wattage of her very al-
luring smile whilst they were totally ignored.

Poppy had always known that other women found
her elder cousin attractive. She could even remember
how, in the days before she had fallen in love with
Chris, she had actually felt angry and jealous herself
if he paid her schoolfriends more attention than he
did her, but those days were gone now, and even
though she registered the assessing look the receptionist gave her as James leant over the desk to speak
to the girl and handed her their passports she was not
affected by it. The receptionist was welcome to him.
She gave a small shudder. She could think of nothing
more loathsome . . . noone more . . .

She tensed as she suddenly realised what the receptionist was saying to James, and hurried towards him,
demanding angrily, 'What does she mean, *our* room?'

The girl was already reaching behind her to hand
James a pass-key. *A* key, Poppy noticed in disbelief.

'James . . .' she urged, but James had already anticipated her and was turning back to the receptionist,
telling her in swift, fluent Italian that there appeared
to have been a mistake, and that they required two
separate rooms.

'No,' the girl denied, shaking her head, picking up
their passports and a list she had in front of her. She
read out carefully, 'Mr and Mrs Carlton,' and then
said, first to Poppy, 'You are Mrs Carlton,' and then
to James, 'and you Mr Carlton.'

'I am Poppy Carlton,' Poppy confirmed, 'but I am
not his wife. We are not married . . . I am not . . . his
wife,' she emphasised.

When the receptionist continued to gaze blankly at her, she turned angrily to James, appealing, 'You tell her, James. Explain...make her understand.'

How could such a mistake have been made? Poppy fumed as she stood back whilst James quickly explained to the receptionist the misunderstanding which seemed to have occurred and asked her to change their booking from one double room to two singles.

Chris's secretary had made the original bookings. She was comfortably middle-aged and extremely efficient and Poppy couldn't believe that she could have made such a mistake. The receptionist had summoned the duty manager at James's request and James was now explaining the situation to him and reiterating the fact that they required two separate rooms.

The duty manager shrugged and shook his head. 'That, I am afraid, is not possible,' he told James. 'The hotel is fully booked for the conference, every room already taken...'

'But they must have somewhere...some room,' Poppy gasped as she heard what he was saying.

'None; there is nowhere,' the duty manager repeated firmly.

'Then we'll just have to find somewhere else to stay,' Poppy burst out.

Her face flushed beneath the withering look that James gave her as he asked her sardonically, 'Where exactly did you have in mind? The nearest town is forty miles away.'

'Then...then I'll just have to...to sleep in the car,' Poppy asserted wildly. 'I—'

'For four days?' James gave her a derisive look. 'Don't be so ridiculous...'

'James, you can't let them do this,' Poppy protested as the duty manager turned away from them to deal with the harassed-looking courier in charge of a party of Japanese businessmen who, from what Poppy could hear of their agitated conversation, had lost not just some luggage *en route* but one member of their party as well. 'Do something.'

'Such as?' James asked, gesturing to the now packed reception area and the press of people demanding attention from the receptionists.

'You've attended conferences before; you know what they're like,' he pointed out. 'The rule is if it can go wrong it will...'

'Maybe, but it's never *gone* wrong before,' Poppy seethed. 'How can they make a mistake like that...? There must be something you can do... Offer to pay them extra... to...'

'Poppy,' James told her, speaking slowly and patiently as though she were a child too young to grasp what he was saying. 'There *are* no empty rooms. Believe me. I just heard one of the receptionists telling another that she's already been forced to give up her staff room and share with someone else on another shift because of overbooking. Believe me, it's either this room or nothing.'

It was on the tip of Poppy's tongue to tell him that if that was the case then there was no way she was staying. But then she remembered how much James would relish her giving him an opportunity to prove how unprofessional she really was and she forced the impulsive words back.

James, taking her acceptance for granted, was already signing the register and taking possession of their pass-cards.

'We might as well find our own way,' he told Poppy. 'God knows how long we'd have to wait for a porter.'

Like her, James was only carrying a briefcase and an overnight bag. She just hoped that the hotel's laundry facilities were better organised and more reliable than its booking system, she reflected angrily as she followed James towards the nearest bank of lifts.

The modern part of the complex had been built around an atrium and as the lift took them upwards they could look down past the open balconies to the greenery and splashing fountains below them.

Although the complex had been given the title of spa it did not actually possess any natural hot springs or spa waters of its own, the term, Poppy suspected, being used in a slightly looser sense to embrace the fact that it offered a wide range of self-indulgent treatments and dietary regimes and holistic alternative therapies.

Their room was on one of the upper floors, the silence as they stepped out of the lift onto the polished marble floor broken only by the hum of the air-conditioning.

'This way,' James instructed her. Their room was halfway down the corridor and Poppy waited whilst James opened the door, and then froze with shock as she followed him inside and stared in white-faced disbelief at the room's one, single, solitary double bed.

A double bed...

She looked at James, then back at the bed, announced flatly, 'I don't believe this...'

'Correct me if I'm wrong, Poppy,' James told her smoothly, 'but, as the company's official translator, wouldn't it normally fall within your field of operations to provide correct foreign translations for those departments which might need them?'

'You know it would,' Poppy agreed irritably. 'But—'

'In that case you would then be the person responsible for providing a correctly worded translation for this booking.'

'If I had been asked for one, yes,' Poppy agreed. 'But—'

'And I think I am also right in saying,' James continued grimly, 'that when this particular booking was made you believed that you would be attending this conference with Chris...'

Poppy stared at him in shocked disbelief as she realised what he was implying.

'Yes, I did think I would be coming here with Chris,' she agreed furiously, 'but that does not mean that I deliberately altered the booking so that Chris and I would be forced to share a room. I had nothing to do with this booking. It was made by fax whilst I was away on holiday, and if you think for one moment that, no matter what...my feelings for...for *anyone*, I would ever stoop to doing something like this...that I would ever try to force...or manipulate a man...any man, but most especially one I...I cared about to—'

She couldn't go on, her words abruptly suspended by the force of her emotions.

'I can't stay here in this room with you,' she protested huskily when she could trust herself to speak again. 'I can't...and I—'

'Stop being so hysterical,' James told her coldly. 'You don't have any choice. Neither of us does. This conference is very important. I've spent months making contact with various international companies who'll be attending it... potential customers, and I don't have time to waste dealing with a hysterical, manipulative idiot who—'

'I did *not* arrange this. It has nothing to do with me,' Poppy protested furiously. 'The last thing I want...I would ever want...is to share a be—a room with you...'

'I believe you,' James told her, adding cuttingly, 'But then you didn't think you would be here with *me*, did you? And, I promise you, Poppy, you're not exactly my ideal choice of bed-mate either. What the hell was that conniving little mind of yours planning? Some kind of emotional blackmail...? A threat to tell Sally that Chris had been sleeping with you if he didn't come across and—'

'*No!*'

Her denial had been as explosive as a blow, Poppy acknowledged as she stared at James in sick disbelief. Did he really think she could... would stoop to something so underhanded as that?

Her mouth twisted bitterly as she made herself look straight into the wintry contempt of his eyes and told him quietly, 'I love Chris, James, and in my book that means putting him first...not wanting to hurt him... Despite what you seem to think, I don't need you to tell me that Chris doesn't feel the same way about me. Do you really think I'd want him on those kinds of terms...? That I'd want any man who...?' She swallowed, unable to go on.

'What I think is that you've become so obsessed
with your so-called love for Chris that you don't know
what's reasonable or rational any more...'

'You're wrong,' Poppy told him, but she could see
from the look on his face that he didn't believe her.

CHAPTER THREE

POPPY exhaled her pent-up breath in an angry hiss of despair, turning away from the panoramic view through the bedroom window in front of her and quickly averting her eyes from the bed.

James was downstairs in the conference hall where he had gone to check that their display stand, which had been shipped out via their Italian agents, had been assembled correctly, and she knew that sooner or later she was going to have to join him. After all, that was why she was here.

Officially, the conference didn't open until the morning but she knew from previous experience that the conference hall would be teeming with people getting ready for the opening.

How had it happened? she wondered miserably. How could such a mistake have occurred and, even worse, how could . . . how dared James imply that she had had anything to do with it, that she had deliberately manipulated things so that she and Chris would be sharing a room?

She had already contemplated refusing to share the bed with him, but the room's furnishings, although elegant, were not particularly comfortable and the marble floor would certainly not make a comfortable bed.

The saving grace was that at least the bed was a good size and there should be no danger of the two of them actually having to sleep close together. If she lay on her side and faced away from him, she might even be able to pretend that James wasn't there at all.

And at least there was one thing she most definitely did not have to worry about. There was no way that James would try to take advantage of the situation or of her. She almost laughed aloud at the very thought.

Years ago, when they had all been children, there had been occasions when they had all holidayed together, and whilst they had never actually shared a bedroom there had been the kind of family intimacy between the cousins which had been natural under such circumstances.

That had been when they were children, though, Poppy acknowledged, and there was a vast difference between a five-year-old and a thirteen-year-old running, dressing gown-clad, between their separate bedrooms and two adults of twenty-two and thirty sharing the intimacy of a bed as well as a bathroom.

The flimsy cotton robe that she had brought with her was hardly as protective or concealing as the thick, fleecy dressing gown that she had worn as a child and... Poppy froze and closed her eyes, cursing herself under her breath as she remembered that the one thing she had decided there was no need for her to bring with her was any kind of nightdress.

Remembering the golden rule of easy travelling— only take what you can carry on and off the plane in your hand luggage—she had kept her packing to the bare minimum... 'Bare' being the operative word, she reflected grimly now.

Normally she was quite happy to sleep in her skin...she preferred it, in fact...but under these circumstances...

Tiredly she ran her hand through her hair. Her skin felt grubby and gritty from travelling and the one thing the room did have, which had impressed her, was a huge walk-in shower.

James wouldn't be in any hurry to return—after all, he would have as little desire to spend any time in her company as she did to spend time in his—and it made sense to take advantage of his absence to have a shower now rather than to wait until he had returned and then suffer the embarrassment of using the bathroom whilst he was there.

Poppy had already unpacked the clothes that she had brought with her and, quickly selecting clean underwear, a fresh shirt and a pair of simple, well-cut silk and linen trousers in her favourite shade of warm cream, she hurried into the bathroom, where she hesitated before leaving the door slightly ajar and then checking to make sure it couldn't swing closed.

As a child she had once been locked in the bathroom at the house of friends of her parents and the small incident had left her with what she knew to be an irrational fear of the same thing ever happening again. Irrational, but strong enough to ensure that she could never actually bring herself to lock herself in any kind of room.

She showered the stickiness of their journey off her skin first before lathering it generously with her favourite shower gel. Poppy rarely wore full-strength perfume, preferring the more subtly fragrant effect of shower gels and body lotions, so that the only way other people could tell that she was wearing any would be if they actually touched her or...

She closed her eyes, clenching them against the hot sting of tears which she told herself were stupidly self-pitying as she recognised the direction her thoughts were taking and the deliberate self-infliction of pain in acknowledging that the only person who could share her awareness of her body's delicate fragrance would have to be someone who was very physically intimate with her...a lover. But she had no lover...no one to love her... He loved someone else...

She knew that she was crying silent, anguished tears as she turned off the shower and soaped her body, too lost in the misery of her own despair to hear the bedroom door opening, so that it wasn't until he thrust open the unlocked bathroom door that she realised that James was back.

For a second neither of them said anything, the only sounds to break the silence being the noise of the dripping shower and her shocked, indrawn breath as the lather that covered her body in creamy ribbons of foam slid off her skin, leaving her sleek and silky and completely naked.

For once Poppy's reactions were the faster, her breath squeezing out of her lungs, her arms lifting to cross over her bare breasts in a gesture that was as instinctively feminine as it was hopelessly inadequate as a means of concealing her, her eyes brilliant with shock as she looked helplessly towards the towel airing on the rail, which was closer to James than it was to her. To reach it she would have to step out of the shower and walk right past him and...

Gritting her teeth and giving him a look of pure, vitriolic loathing, she prepared to do so. He had seen just about all there was to see of her now, after all, she decided grimly, and if he thought that she was going to stand there cowering whilst he enjoyed her embarrassment...

But, to her amazement, as she took a step forward he suddenly reached for the towel, his expression difficult to read, his eyes darkening, his mouth hardening in a way that made her tense and watch him.

Being the recipient of James's anger and contempt was nothing new to her, but on this occasion, she decided indignantly as he suddenly reached for the towel and almost threw it at her, she had no idea what on earth she was supposed to have done to merit the glittering fury she could see in his eyes.

'Cover yourself up, for God's sake, will you, Poppy?' he instructed her harshly. 'You aren't a child any more, even if emotionally you do still behave like one.'

'You should have knocked,' she told him fiercely as she wrapped the towel around her body.

'You should have locked the door,' James countered, 'or are we still playing at make-believe and fantasising that somehow I'm going to turn into Chris...?'

'I don't *have* that much imagination,' Poppy told him bitterly, and added for good measure, 'No one could have...'

'Be careful, Poppy,' James warned her coldly, 'otherwise I might just forget that you are still, after all, my cousin and that as such—'

'I might be your cousin,' Poppy interrupted him recklessly, 'but that still doesn't give you the right to come barging in here, nor to treat me as though...as though I'm some kind of child you—'

'No?' James stopped her. 'Then how would you like me to treat you...?'

There was a note in his voice that made Poppy stiffen and turn her head to look over her shoulder

at him, at first in query and then in shocked disbelief
as she saw the way he was looking at her.

She had always known that James was a man with
an extremely high-voltage sexual charisma—she had
heard other women telling her so often enough after
all—but to be suddenly and unexpectedly subjected
to a thorough sexual scrutiny of such blistering heat
and savagery that it virtually stripped the thick fluffy
towel from her body and left her feeling far more
naked and vulnerable than she had felt when she had
actually been naked was unexpectedly shocking.

As she followed the way he was slowly and oh, so
deliberately studying every line of her body, every
curve, every hollow, in some satanic way, it was almost
as though she could see herself through his eyes, see
what he was seeing as he visually stripped her and
examined her as cruelly and callously and dehuman-
isingly as though her body were a piece of mer-
chandise that he had every right to assess and value
and reject.

When he had finally finished his assessment and
his eyes met hers, she had no defence left against the
shock of what he had done, no barriers strong enough
to put up.

She couldn't make a sound . . . couldn't shed a tear,
couldn't express in any way her sense of outrage and
humiliation, her feeling of shocked pain at the way
he had assessed her as a woman and then dismissed
her. No, not a woman, she decided as she tried to
swallow past the hard lump blocking her throat. Not
a woman but just a piece of flesh, a body . . . a thing
without any right to emotions or needs of her own,
without any right to self-respect or . . .

As she finally managed to break eye contact with him and find her voice, she told him croakily, her voice creaking under the weight of her fury, 'I've often wondered why you've never settled down, James...married...had a family...but now I know. If that's how you see women...if that's how you treat your women—'

'You know nothing about *my* women,' James interrupted her harshly, and then added contemptuously as he moved closer to her and took hold of her chin in a grip that she couldn't manage to break, 'Let's face it, Poppy, you know nothing about *being* a woman...what it means...how it feels...'

'In your opinion,' Poppy spat at him, finally managing to wrench herself out of his grip. 'But I'll tell you one thing I do know, James, and that's that you're the last man I'd want to show me...the last man I'd *let* show me,' she added emphatically.

'Don't tempt me,' James responded grimly as he turned towards the door, pausing only to warn her, 'Don't challenge me, Poppy; you can't win and you won't like the consequences... I came to warn you that we're likely to be in for a chaotic few days. The hotel seems to have overestimated its ability to handle the mechanics of the conference and so they've had to suspend room service.

'This evening's dinner is due to be served at eight-thirty and if you want something to eat I'd advise you to make sure you're downstairs early. I've got a strong suspicion that we aren't the only ones with problems.

'I overheard someone else's conversation whilst I was talking to our agent and it seems that some of the rooms which should have been ready for occupation aren't.

'I've still got a few things I need to iron out—' he glanced at his watch '—so I'll meet you downstairs at eight.' He paused for a moment before adding silkily, 'Unless, of course, you feel you're going to want another shower...'

Giving him an angry glare, Poppy started to step past him, but he stopped her, reaching out and picking up the clean underwear that she had forgotten and handing it to her.

'Don't forget these, will you...?'

Snatching them out of his hand, flushing as she saw the way he was looking at her perfectly respectable but admittedly rather plain, no-nonsense bra and briefs, she couldn't resist saying contemptuously, 'I suppose a man like you prefers something... something in scarlet satin.'

For a moment she thought that he wasn't going to bother replying, but as she turned towards the door she saw his mouth starting to curl slightly at the corners and his eyes glint with the same dangerous, glittering mockery which she had learned long ago presaged his more razor-sharp attacks on her pride.

'Satin, yes,' he drawled tauntingly. 'Scarlet...no, never. But you're way out of date with your ideas of what a man finds sexy in a woman these days, Poppy, or of what a woman might do in that department to turn him on. No wonder you couldn't get Chris interested.

'Next time—if there ever *is* a next time...or a next man—try baiting your trap a little more cleverly. A seductive little whisper in a very public place that underneath the very respectable skirt you've got on you're wearing...nothing...works wonders, or so I've been told...'

'You're disgusting,' Poppy told him furiously, her cheeks burning as she realised what he meant. 'And, for your information, I would never—'

'Oh, no, Poppy,' James corrected her mock-gently, 'I'm not disgusting, but you most certainly are naïve...very naïve.

'Now, didn't you say something about coming here to work? I want you to send a fax for me, please. I hope that your Japanese is as good as your mother claims. I've just been talking to one of the German groups; their linguist spent two years in Tokyo...'

'Probably as a geisha,' Poppy muttered disrespectfully under her breath as James finally walked out of the bathroom and left her in peace to get dressed.

It didn't matter that she was his cousin and that there had been countless occasions in their shared childhood when he had seen her naked. She could even remember once suffering the indignity of having her seven-year-old self stripped of her torn and filthy clothes, summarily dumped into the bath and virtually scrubbed clean by him at the same time as he delivered a lecture to her on what was likely to happen to her if her mother found out that she had deliberately ignored her instructions that she was not to play in the stream at the foot of their shared holiday-cottage garden.

Then she had foolishly actually been grateful to James...and, even more ridiculously, seen him as her saviour... Now she knew better, she decided.

James had been right about the chaos, was Poppy's first thought as she waited for him to join her in the crowded foyer as they had arranged. She had already talked to several other people whom she had recognised from other conferences and they had confirmed what James had already told her.

It seemed that the hotel manager had overestimated their ability to cope with something as complex as organising such a large-scale event.

'They say that two of the chefs have already left and that they've had to bribe the others to stay,' a German sales manager whom Poppy had met at Frankfurt the previous year had confided to her.

At the time, Chris had teased her gently that Gunther Weiner was obviously attracted to her, and as she'd listened to him she had wished achingly that it were Chris's attraction for her that they were discussing and not another man's...

She heard Gunther asking her if she had again attended the conference with her cousin.

'Yes,' she told him absently, her attention on James, whom she could see making his way towards them.

Excusing herself to Gunther, she went to meet him.

'Who was that?' James demanded curtly, looking over her shoulder at Gunther.

When she told him he demanded, 'What did he want?'

The aggression in his voice surprised her. 'Well, not our company secrets, James,' she told him, enjoying mocking him as he constantly did her, adding with relish, 'Hard though you may find it to believe, *he* is more interested in me.'

She looked at him, waiting for him to come back at her with some typically derogatory response, and then looked curiously across the room to see what was occupying his attention and causing anger to tighten his mouth to a hairline, but he still seemed to be watching Gunther walking away from them.

Dinner, predictably, was a chaotic and hurried affair, although the food was surprisingly good—not that she had very much of an appetite.

Once they had finished eating James announced that he had some business he wanted to attend to and left her to her own devices. Poppy decided that she might as well explore the rest of the hotel.

The brochure had stressed the benefits of the spa, highlighting the various treatments available, but upon enquiry Poppy discovered that the delay in completion of the building work had meant that most of these facilities were not yet up and running.

There was the Jacuzzi, the sauna and steam room, the gym and the swimming pool, the receptionist informed her, although no one was allowed to use them after ten o'clock in the evening.

It was already gone ten but, nevertheless, Poppy decided that she might as well take a look. The brochure had shown photographs of the swimming pool and Jacuzzi area which had included views through the floor-to-ceiling glass wall on one whole side, looking straight out across the sheer rock-face to the spectacular view beyond it. And, even though it was now dark, the moon was almost full, and should shed enough light to illuminate at least some of the view.

Poppy found her way to the sports centre quite easily. The swimming pool was clearly marked, set in a circular, enclosed area with a raised platform overlooking the now covered pool on one side and allowing a view through the huge expanse of glass she recognised from the brochure on the other.

The remaining two walls, from what she could see in the dim lighting, had been painted with frescos, and a columned walkway led from the pool towards

the Jacuzzi and, beyond it, to what she presumed to
be another entrance.

As she paused to study the frescos with interest, she
heard a sudden sound from the Jacuzzi. Lifting her
head, Poppy stared curiously towards it. There appeared to be two people in the water. As she watched,
she heard a feminine giggle followed by a soft shushing
sound and then male laughter, accompanied by the
rhythmic sound of the water moving, as if... as if...

Poppy could feel her face starting to flush as she
suddenly realised what was happening...what she had
interrupted. They were not, as she had originally
thought, two people simply illicitly using the Jacuzzi
after hours but a pair of lovers who had obviously
decided to try out for themselves the pool's aphro-
disiac effect, and then, having discovered that it was
not in operation, had patently decided that they might
as well make use of...make love in it, after all.

Even though she knew that there was no way they
could see her, Poppy felt her face burning an even
deeper red as she heard one of them—the woman, she
suspected—giving a small, soft moan.

Quickly turning on her heel, she started to walk
away. Her face was still burning by the time she
reached her room...their room, she acknowledged
as she took off her jacket and saw thankfully that
there was no sign of James. And she decided that she
might as well prepare for bed whilst she had the place
to herself.

Seeing that couple making love, hearing them,
knowing what they were doing hadn't just embarrassed her, it had also brought back all the pain of
knowing that Chris was lost to her... Her throat and
eyes ached with the weight of the tears that she re-

fused to allow herself to cry. The last thing she needed now was for James to come back and find her in tears, and yet, as she prepared for bed, her heart ached with the pain of her loss, her mind filled with feverish, tormented thoughts and mental images.

What was it like to have your love...your need...your desire for a man reciprocated? To know that he wanted you? To feel his desire for you? To know that you had the freedom to reach out and touch him, to share every sensual and emotional intimacy with him? To love him and be loved by him?

Her hands trembling, Poppy pulled on the robe she had unpacked earlier. Used to sleeping naked, as she climbed into the large bed she grimaced at the unfamiliar drag of the fabric against her skin, already disliking the cumbersome restriction of the cloth. As she reached out to switch off the bedside light she was already yawning.

Poppy was having the most wonderful dream. In it all her heartache and loneliness had gone, melted away by the loving warmth of the man whose arms held her so tightly, the man whose body shielded and protected her own, the man who whispered to her that he loved her and that he had always loved her, that he would always love her...

A delicious thrill of pleasure ran through her as she moved even closer to him, pressing her body against his, enjoying the satin warmth of his skin against her own, her senses glorying in the nearness of him, in her freedom to share such intimacy with him, to show him her love.

She had known him for a long, long time...loved him for a long time, but this familiarity, instead of lessening the intensity of the pleasure that lapped at her body in soft, warm waves, only increased it. It gave her a sense of security, an ability to shed her inhibitions and to show her feelings, her desire for him freely and openly, to reach out and touch him, to smooth her fingertips over his skin.

In her sleep Poppy made a soft, contented sound of pleasure as she snuggled closer to James, burrowing against his body, unaware of what she was doing and of the fact that the robe that she had so carefully and resentfully put on earlier was now lying on the floor where she had thrown it, having finally, in her sleep, given in to the irritation of its unaccustomed feel against her skin and pulled it off.

James, disturbed by the sensual movement of her body against his, woke up, cursing silently as he reached out to push her away and put some distance between them.

In her sleep Poppy protested about the removal of the warmth which had been giving her so much pleasure, the body which had felt so good against her own, the man who had made her feel so protected and loved, and she protested both verbally and physically, muttering a husky plea for him to come back and, at the same time, resisting his attempts to put some distance between them, wriggling her body back against his and curling her fingers possessively around his wrist.

'Poppy...' James warned her savagely under his breath.

He had always prided himself on his self-control. The need to conceal his own feelings had been something he had learned young—he had had no other option when his father had died or when ... But there came a point when no amount of self-control was enough, when no man...

He took hold of Poppy's shoulder, shaking her, but her eyes remained tightly closed, her body locked in sleep. In the moonlit room he could see the rich tumble of her hair, silk against silk where it lay against her skin; he reached out and touched it, smoothing the tangled tendrils.

Poppy smiled sensuously as she breathed in the familiar scent of his skin. She moved her head and touched her lips to his shoulder, sighing blissfully as she absorbed the taste of him, opening her mouth so that she could touch him with her tongue.

James went completely still and then slowly lifted his hand from her hair, but it was too late—had been too late, he suspected, since he had walked into the bedroom and seen her discarded robe lying on the floor and known that she was sleeping naked.

'Poppy.'

As he said her name he gathered up his strength to push her away and instead discovered that he was actually gathering her closer—so close that they were lying body to body—and that the hands which should have been holding her away from him were actually moving urgently over her skin, following the narrow contours of her back, the feminine curve of her waist and hips, the smooth roundness of her buttocks.

Her lips were still touching his skin, and against his body he could feel the excited thud of her heartbeat.

If she woke up now she would feel the equally aroused pounding of his, and the even more betraying arousal of another part of him. If he had any sense, any thought of self-preservation he would...

James bent his head and slid one hand into Poppy's hair, tilting her face up to meet his, covering her mouth with his.

When Poppy woke up she discovered that she was being kissed in the most sensual, demanding and exciting way that she had ever known, her whole body responding to the hungry male pressure of the mouth caressing hers, the male hand that held her locked against him so that their bodies fitted together as exactly and perfectly as two separate pieces of one complete whole.

As she breathed in dizzily, she felt her breasts swell and press against his chest, his body moving to accommodate the movement of hers, the sensation of his skin dragging slightly against hers so shockingly erotic that she trembled and moved more urgently against him, wanting to repeat it, wanting to feel him against her—

She wanted to feel *all* of him against her, she recognised longingly as she moved her body pleadingly against his, trying to seek even closer contact with him, needing to feel the sensual roughness of his body hair against her, wanting more, much, much more than the tormenting male heat and hardness of his aroused body, which, for some reason, he was allowing merely to rest lightly against hers when she wanted . . .

Poppy tried to show him exactly what it was she wanted by opening her mouth under his and kissing him passionately at the same time as she moved her hips against him, pressed her breasts against him, arched her spine and made soft keening sounds of need as she opened her legs and rubbed her body hungrily against his.

It was unfair of him to withhold himself from her like this when he knew how much she wanted him, how much she needed him, how much she loved him.

Poppy's soft moans of protest turned to sharper sounds of delight when he suddenly responded to the urgent little movements of her body, thrusting his thigh between hers and making her shiver from head to foot with pleasure at the sensation of his hair-roughened flesh moving against the silky softness of hers.

It must feel good to him as well, she realized, because now he kissed her much more passionately, thrilling her with the husky growl of her name as he held her face in his hands and circled her lips with his tongue-tip, using the weight of his body and the pressure of his hands to make her lie completely still while he teased her with the movement of his tongue and an even more erotic movement of his hips to the point where she couldn't be still any more and her body physically and very visibly shuddered in uncontrollable response to what he was doing to her.

For how many years had she longed for him like this, dreamed of him holding her like this, wanting her like this, loving her like this...? All the feelings and needs she had suppressed surged up inside her in a flood-tide that swept her with it, drowning out everything but her need and her desire.

'No,' she protested in a husky whisper when his mouth left hers and he lifted her wrist to kiss the delicate, blue-veined skin. 'Not there, not there,' she urged; her body burned, ached, hurt almost with her need for him.

The memory of the couple that she had discovered in the Jacuzzi made her shudder, the blood burning up under her skin as he lifted his mouth from her wrist and asked her thickly, 'Not there... Where, then, Poppy? Where...?'

His voice sounded different, deeper, rougher, much more raw and masculine somehow, and she shivered again as she recognised why. It was the voice of a man who was aroused...who wanted her...

'Here,' she told him, placing his hand against her breast, holding her breath almost as she looked first into his eyes and then at his mouth. His mouth...

'Here,' she heard him repeat softly, and the feel of his mouth against her, slowly caressing her nipple, was almost more than she could bear. Her body, her senses weren't equipped to handle so much pleasure, and yet not to have it would have been a loss she could not bear to contemplate.

'And this one?' she heard him asking her hoarsely as he slowly released one breast to turn to the other, lingering over a delicate exploration of it whilst he waited for her response.

Did he really need to ask? Poppy wondered feverishly, but she still said the words, whispering them jerkily as she told him, 'Yes... oh, yes... yes...'

This time the sensation of his suckling on her nipple actually made her cry out in exquisite, sharp pleasure—a high, bitter-sweet sound that made him take hold of her so tightly that she could feel the bite of his fingers against the flesh of her waist, his mouth moving on her so demandingly that she wasn't sure if she could endure such intense pleasure.

She could feel the sexual tension that he was creating within her coiling and stretching like a tautly drawn cord from her breasts right the way down her body so that her womb ached as hotly as her breasts and her need for him drenched her skin in a moist heat.

And somehow, as though he knew how and where that cord ran and why, he started to trace its pathway along her body until the sensation of his mouth moving over her made her tremble wildly and cry out to him that she couldn't bear any more, that the intensity of what she was feeling was too much for her to endure, that she felt as though the terrible pressure of her desire for him was somehow going to tear her apart, destroy her self-control, make her...

Her eyes wet with tears, she tried to tell him how not even all the years of wanting this, of aching for him had prepared her for the intensity of what she was experiencing...how she had never known that just looking at his body, so strongly and powerfully male, would fill her with a need that she couldn't control and that touching him and being touched by him would quicken her pulse and her heartbeat until her whole body shook with the violence of their excitement.

'I never knew it would be like this,' she told him helplessly. 'All these years and I never knew it could be...it would be...'

She felt his own hand tremble as he cupped her face and kissed her gently, his mouth absorbing the dampness of her emotional tears.

'No,' he told her thickly, 'but I did.' And then he was kissing her as Poppy had never known that it was possible to be kissed, so that the pressure of his mouth and the thrust of his tongue was an act of possession as intimate and shockingly intense as the final act of possession itself.

His hands swept down over her body, his thigh nudging hers apart, his body so fully aroused that her hot flood of eager response was shot through with small, bright sparks of apprehensive female awe and female pride at knowing that she was the one who had aroused him so intensely, that she was the one he wanted, the one...

The touch of his hand against her sex as he stroked her swamped her with hot forked-lightning darts of pleasure, making her move her body closer to him, making her...

She reached down for his hand, her voice unsteady with emotion as she told him, 'No... not that... it's you I want... you.' And then, as her control broke when he moved over her then into her, she cried out, 'Oh, yes... yes. Oh, Chris, I want you so much—'

'Chris!'

The name was snarled at her, hurled back at her, the exquisite, unbearable, unimaginable pleasure of the slow penetration of her body by his ceasing in mid-thrust as she felt him grasp her shoulders and then lift one hand to her face as he demanded savagely, 'Open your eyes, Poppy. I am *not* Chris.'

No, of course he wasn't Chris. How could she ever have imagined that he was, deceived herself that he was, believed that he was? Poppy agonised in shocked self-awareness as she looked up into the icy, furious glare of James's eyes.

Her teeth started to chatter, her brain seized by a nausea so intense that it paralysed any logical thought.

Like someone in a trance she stared up at James. James, who had touched her more intimately than any other man had ever done. James, who had made her body feel... want. James, who...

He had started to withdraw from her but her body had no intention of giving up on the pleasure that his had promised it; her body had no conscience, no awareness, no knowledge, after all, of Chris as its lover; her *body* only knew the pleasure that *James* had given it and as it tightened and clung to his and she heard herself uttering a surprisingly fierce and strong, 'No,' Poppy's eyes registered her own confusion and disbelief.

It was Chris she loved, Chris she wanted, she protested inwardly to her wayward flesh, but it didn't want to listen to her; it knew no Chris, it only knew that it wanted...must have what it had been promised, and as James started again to withdraw from her Poppy found that somehow, without knowing how, she was actually moving against him, reaching out to hold onto him, imploring him with words which she would once have denied that she could ever bring herself to say to any man, no matter how much she loved him—much less this man.

'No, please don't... I want you... I want you... Oh, please... I want you so much...'

The words became a husky, rhythmic accompaniment to the increasingly urgent movements of her body as it tried frantically to draw him deeper within itself, tried and, unbelievably, it seemed, succeeded, Poppy realised in dizzy, trembling relief. She was too caught up in the intensity of her body's drive towards its sensual goal to be able to concentrate on anything other than the pleasure of that deepening sense of fullness within her; she was so caught up in it that nothing, nothing could be allowed to bring an end to that sensation of heady, addictive pleasure.

She wanted him, needed him, ached for him too much to care about what he was actually saying as his body began to move within hers again.

'No, you don't, Poppy; you want my brother. But I'm the one you've got. I'm the one who's touched you, caressed you, aroused you, shown you . . . taught you what it is to feel real physical desire, instead of dreaming some idealised dream; and I'm the one—'

When he heard her cry out he stopped speaking abruptly, his hand tangling in her hair so that he could look into her eyes before she could defend herself from him and close them.

The pain, so sharp that it had been responsible for her high-pitched, shocked cry, had gone as quickly as it had come, but the ache which had preceded it had not, nor the need and the slight trembling of her body. And the quickened pace of her breathing had nothing to do with any fear or desire for him to stop.

He was doing it deliberately, Poppy guessed. Having deliberately aroused her, he now wanted to humiliate and punish her by stopping and . . .

Angry tears filled her eyes as she glared back at him. 'You can't do this to me,' she protested frantically. 'You can't leave me now, without . . . You can't . . .'

She didn't see his expression before, without warning, his lids dropped, his lashes veiling it from her.

He wasn't looking at her face any more, Poppy recognised, but he was looking at her body, at her breasts in point of fact, and as he looked he lifted one hand and cupped one of them, stroking the taut nipple whilst he asked her softly, 'I can't what, Poppy?'

She couldn't answer him; the way he was touching her had galvanised her whole body into a shuddering shock of hot, fluid reaction.

'James... James...' she heard herself pleading achingly.

'Say it... Say it... Say my name,' she heard him telling her softly. 'Tell me again how much you want me, Poppy; tell me again what it is you want, Poppy...*who* it is you want. My God, if you knew...'

Poppy knew that she should stop him, tell him that she hated him, loathed him, detested him, but she also knew that she wouldn't, couldn't; she was blind, deaf and dumb to everything but the urgency he had generated within her. If he stopped making love to her now, without...before...she thought that she would die.

'I want you... I want you...' she whispered obediently, her breath catching in her throat as she responded to the deep rhythm that he was slowly imposing on her—felt it, clung to it, ached for it and finally, as she heard herself cry out his name, abandoned herself totally to it, letting him drive her beyond the safe, known edge of her universe and out into the void that lay beyond it, carried along by wave after wave of pleasure and the hot pulsing of his own release within her.

Her body was still trembling with the aftershock of it many minutes later when she fell into an exhausted sleep.

James watched her for several seconds, his mouth bitter, before turning his back on her and putting as much distance between them as he could.

CHAPTER FOUR

POPPY woke up reluctantly, an ingrained sense of self-preservation warning her that it was safer to cling to the protective blanket of sleep, that she wouldn't like what she was going to have to face when she opened her eyes and remembered what had happened.

She didn't. The shock of the appalling flashbacks that poured over her in an icy deluge of self-knowledge made her sit bolt upright in bed and exclaim out aloud, 'No! I couldn't have... I didn't...'

But she knew, all too well, that she had. The space in the bed next to her where James must have slept was now, thankfully, empty.

Where was he? He must have gone down to the conference hall, she decided.

'And you'd just better get yourself up and dressed and ready to face him when he comes back,' she warned herself grimly.

Face him! The mere thought of doing so was enough to make her stomach churn wildly and her body burn with shamed heat.

Quickly she scrambled out of bed; her body ached slightly in a way that was new and unfamiliar, the self-conscious heat scorching her skin becoming searingly intense as all too vivid and detailed unwanted memories of the way she had behaved, the things she had said the previous night returned.

As she stood in the shower she could see where James's passion was already beginning to bruise her skin—the passion *she* had urged him, *begged* him to show her.

'No. I didn't... I couldn't have...' Poppy moaned, but she knew that she had, and, worse, she knew that he must know it too.

'I thought he was Chris,' she whispered helplessly in defence of her body's physical treachery, its undeniable and inescapable, illogical and unbearable sexual response to him.

By the time she was showered and dressed it was almost eight o'clock. She ought to go downstairs and have some breakfast, Poppy acknowledged, but the last thing she felt like doing was eating. No, not the last thing, she admitted mercilessly; that was having to see James, having to look at him and know what had happened between them, having to...

She tensed as she heard the bedroom door open and saw James walk in.

Despite her determination not to do so, she could feel herself starting to flush, her eyes looking everywhere but at him.

'I... I was just on my way down to breakfast,' she told him untruthfully, hurrying towards the door.

'Not yet. There's something I want to say to you—'

'No!' The speed and vehemence with which she blurted out her panicky denial betrayed her all too clearly, Poppy knew, as James reached out and took hold of her wrist, swinging her round so that he was standing between her and the door.

'Let me go,' she demanded fiercely. 'I want you—'

'So you told me—last night,' James interrupted her, watching her mercilessly as the colour came and went in her face and her body stiffened as though he had struck her.

'No,' she whispered in denial. 'That ... that wasn't you. I ...'

Her whole body trembled as she fought for something to say, some reasonable and logical explanation of what she had done, what she had said, what she had felt. But, finally acknowledging that there was none, she reached desperately and dangerously for the only thing she had left, picking it up and hurling it at him with all the force of her pent-up, tangled emotions.

'What happened last night wasn't ... It didn't ... I didn't ... I thought you were Chris ... I was dreaming about him and when ... You must have known that I thought you were him,' she cried out defensively. 'You must have known that I would never ... That ...'

She stopped abruptly as she saw the dangerous warning expression on James's face, her stomach dropping sickeningly as she realised how angry he was.

'Go on,' he invited her softly. 'You were saying that you thought I was Chris, that you were dreaming about Chris, but you weren't asleep when we made love, were you, Poppy? You knew very well who it was, who was holding you ... touching you, pleasuring you,' he told her tauntingly, 'even if you do claim now that you wanted it to be my brother ...'

'I ... I believed that you were your brother,' Poppy lied doggedly, driven into a corner by his refusal to allow her the secure defence she so desperately needed. 'I wanted—'

'You wanted me,' James told her bluntly. 'Even if you do prefer to lie to yourself now. You can deceive yourself all you like, Poppy, but you won't deceive me... I was the one who—'

'I was pretending that you were Chris,' Poppy told him frantically, unable to listen to any more. 'I—'

She stopped abruptly as she saw the ominous white line of fury deepen around James's mouth, her stomach knotting into tight cords of anxious dread.

'I see... You *pretended* I was Chris... You *pretended* I was my brother, did you, my cheating little virgin...?' His eyes dropped to her mouth and then lower, caressing the whole of her body in a hatefully knowing way that made her skin burn as though all the flames of hell were consuming it.

Her body trembled as he drawled, 'But then, of course, you aren't a virgin any longer, are you, Poppy?' And he took her by surprise by roughly jerking her towards him, holding her by her upper arms, his body so close to her own that she could feel its angry heat, and she was shaken, driven into a state of shockingly unexpected, aching weakness.

Fighting to deny what her body was frantically trying to tell her, desperate to ignore the tormenting clamour of the need it refused to understand that it couldn't be allowed even to *feel*, never mind acknowledge or openly demonstrate, she was barely aware of the furious tension in James's voice and eyes as he told her savagely, 'And I can tell you this much— no matter how much you might want to deny it now, it was *me* you wanted last night, Poppy, *me* you begged to hold you and touch you... to take you and fill you with my body, to—'

'No...' Poppy protested shrilly. 'No, that's not true... I thought you were someone else... It was Chris I wanted, not you...' she told him piteously.

'That wasn't what you were saying last night,' James reminded her brutally. '"I want you... I want you..."' he mimicked her breathlessly, making her cringe as he caught so devastatingly the note of aching hunger and need she clearly recognised as being her own.

'You knew I thought you were Chris,' she told him. 'You must have done. You know how much I love him. You should have stopped... Why didn't you?'

'Why? Because I'm a man,' he told her callously. 'And when a woman makes herself available sexually to a man, comes on to him, urges him, pleads with him and begs him the way you were doing with me last night...'

He paused and looked at her, then told her grimly, 'If you're looking for an apology, Poppy, or even a defence, I'm afraid you're not going to get one. I gave you what you asked for. What happened between us last night happened because—'

'Because I believed you were your brother,' Poppy interrupted him passionately.

'No,' James corrected her mercilessly. 'You may have wanted me to be Chris... needed me to be him... but you certainly knew that I wasn't. You knew—'

'Stop it, stop it...' Poppy demanded. 'I don't want to talk about it any more. I just want to forget that the whole thing happened,' she told him sickly.

'And you think I don't?' James challenged her brutally. 'You think I *like* knowing that you used *me* as a substitute for my brother, that you vented on me all your pent-up, virginal frustration at not being able to have him?'

The way he was speaking to her shocked Poppy into white-faced silence. James might, in the past, have been unkind to her, might have been angry with her, but he had never, ever been so sexually explicit with her, nor so...so...

'What, nothing to say for yourself?' he demanded bitingly.

'I... It wasn't like that,' Poppy protested, ashen-faced. 'You're making it sound as though...as though I was the one...as though it was me who...'

'Well, wasn't it?' James asked her. 'You say you want to forget the whole thing happened. Well, let's just hope that we'll both be allowed to do just that...'

The note of warning in his voice made Poppy raise her head and look at him directly for the first time since he had entered the room.

His eyes were as cold as the Arctic Ocean and just as cruelly destructive.

'What...what do you mean?' she asked him nervously.

'Use your head, Poppy,' James advised her grimly. 'Last night, at your insistence, we made...had sex, and surely even you aren't naïve enough to have forgotten that there could be...consequences of our...intimacy?'

'Consequences...' Poppy faltered in a stricken voice as she realised what he meant. 'No,' she protested in panic. 'There couldn't... We couldn't...'

'Oh yes, there could,' James corrected her roughly, 'and we most certainly did, if my memory serves me right. And, whilst I've never had occasion to put them to the test, I have no reason to doubt the efficiency of my reproductive organs and last night they—'

'Stop it...stop it...' Poppy begged torturedly, covering her face with her hands as she sobbed. 'You're just trying to frighten me. I can't be... You can't have...'

She heard James laughing savagely at her as she uncovered her face to look at him, his mouth twisted in contempt.

'How modest,' he jeered. 'You can't even bring yourself to say the words, can you? How modest...how proper...and, my God, how inappropriate... Shall I tell you what you said to me last night, what you asked me for?' he demanded mercilessly. 'Shall I repeat for you the words you said to me...the way you urged me, *begged* me to fill you with—?'

'No...no...' Poppy moaned. 'I keep telling you it was a mistake...'

'A mistake?' James shook his head. 'Oh, no...it wasn't *a* mistake,' he told her, 'it was *your* mistake, Poppy. Your mistake.'

He released her so unexpectedly that she staggered slightly, her legs shockingly weak, but when James would have reached out to steady her she pushed him away angrily, fighting to suppress the tears she desperately needed to cry.

'I don't know how I could ever have believed that you were Chris,' Poppy cried out in anguish. 'You are nothing like him—nothing. Chris is kind and gentle; he's...he would never—'

'Never what?' James interrupted her savagely. 'Never arouse you the way I did, never make you want him the way you wanted me, never make you feel, experience, *know* what it really is to be a woman? Is that what you were going to say, Poppy?'

'No,' she denied vehemently.

'No,' James agreed crushingly. 'You aren't capable of being that honest with yourself, are you? *You* prefer the delusion of your cosy, pretty, girlish dream. Well, try being even more honest with yourself, Poppy. Try telling yourself that if you had been in bed with Chris the reason you would have woken up this morning still in your virginally intact state would have been, quite simply, because he didn't want you.'

'And *you* did,' Poppy challenged him shakily, desperately trying to use her anger to protect herself from the pain of acknowledging the truth of his words.

'*I* wanted *a* woman,' James told her cruelly, 'and you made yourself available. I'm not the man to look a gift-horse in the mouth...'

'You do surprise me,' Poppy flashed back with heavy sarcasm. 'I never thought of you as a man who'd be satisfied with a woman who really wanted another man...'

'Who says I was satisfied?' James taunted her. 'If you really think that your immature, adolescent fumblings came anywhere near to giving *me* satisfaction, you've got a hell of a lot to learn—only next time don't expect me to do the teaching.'

'Don't worry, I shan't,' Poppy told him furiously, but inside her anger was already draining away, leaving her feeling sick and empty and not just shamed by her inexplicable behaviour in bed with James, but also vulnerably conscious of the sexual inexperience he had mocked her for.

She longed for the ability to make some witty, crushing remark—the kind of remark she could imagine her friend Star making, which would leave her the victor of their verbal confrontation—but Poppy knew that she simply didn't have either the strength or the energy to find one.

From now on, for the rest of her life, no matter what else might happen to her, each and every time she looked at James she was going to remember just what had happened between them and how she...

'I don't care what it takes or where I have to sleep tonight—I am not going to share that bed with you again,' she told him shakily.

The smile he gave her was as cruel as a hunting wolf's—a baring of his teeth almost that made her feel that he would like nothing more than to savage and destroy her.

'What's wrong?' he asked her silkily. 'Afraid that you might discover that it isn't really Chris you want after all and that your body—?'

'No...' Poppy denied quickly—too quickly? she wondered miserably as she saw the look in James's eyes. That wasn't the reason why she didn't want to share that bed with him for a second night, she reassured herself as she made her way down to the conference hall. Of course it wasn't. How could it be?

She knew that it was another man she had really wanted, another body she had really yearned and ached for even if...even though...

She swallowed painfully, unable to deny the unwanted and tormentingly vivid memory she had of looking into James's eyes, of knowing who he was and still wanting, still saying...

'Hey, are you all right?'

Poppy realised that she had actually closed her eyes and walked right into Gunther as she heard the concern in the young German's voice and opened them to see him looking anxiously at her.

'I'm sorry,' she apologised huskily. 'I was just thinking about . . . something . . .'

'There is no need to apologise,' he told her with a charming smile. 'I was indeed hoping that I might have the chance to talk with you today—'

'Don't tell me you want my services as a linguist?' Poppy teased, responding to the warmth in his smile and only too glad to have something, some*one* to take her mind off James and the appalling events of the previous night. 'If you do, I certainly shan't believe you,' she added. 'Your English is very good.'

'No . . . not that,' he assured her. 'What I wanted to ask was if you would have dinner with me this evening . . .'

Have dinner with him. Poppy gave him a bewitchingly dazzling smile.

'I'd love to,' she told him fervently and honestly. *Anything*, she felt; right now she would be grateful for anything and *anyone* who kept her away from James.

'Poppy, if you've quite finished socialising . . .'

James's voice cracked between them like a whip, making Poppy spin round guiltily, her nervous, 'James,' causing Gunther to look slightly puzzled as he watched her.

'We are here to work,' James reminded her curtly. 'I've got a meeting with a consortium of Japanese buyers in fifteen minutes and I'll need you there to translate, and there are several points I need to run through with you first.'

'I'll be with you in a moment, James,' Poppy told him, trying to stand her ground instead of tamely giving in to the command she had heard in his voice.

She might be his cousin and an employee of the company but she was still her own person, still had her rights. Tilting her chin, she looked away from him and back to Gunther and told him clearly, 'I'd love to have dinner with you tonight, Gunther. Would eight o'clock be all right...?'

Instead of walking away and giving her the privacy to complete her conversation with the young German, James had waited for her like a jailer, determined not to let her get away, she decided angrily as she fell into step beside him and they made their way through the crush towards their own stand.

'If it's his bed you're thinking of sharing tonight, Poppy,' James warned her cynically as he took hold of her arm and guided her through the surging throng, 'I should warn you that you won't get much privacy, nor much bed space. The hotel management have already had to put an extra bed in the room he's booked into as a result of their overbooking!'

'How dare you say that?' Poppy hissed furiously at him, her face burning. She couldn't bear the way he was making her feel so...so cheap...so... 'Just because...just because I... Just because of what happened last night,' she told him in a breathless rush, 'that doesn't mean that I'm now going to go to...to have sex with...with anyone...'

'Really? You do surprise me...' James told her sardonically. 'After all, if you haven't got the scruples not to use one man in place of another, I shouldn't have thought—'

Smack!

Through the tears clouding her eyes, Poppy could see the hazy dark red outline of her open-handed slap against the lean tautness of James's face. She stared at it in shocked, silent horror, unable to believe what she had done, unable to believe the anger, the lack of self-control, the sheer weight of misery and self-disgust which had driven her to overreact in such a way.

As the crowd pressed and surged around them, she was conscious only of James and the frightening stillness of his body, the icy coldness of his eyes, the tension of the coiled strength within him that menaced and held her in paralysed thrall.

'How very predictable and old-fashioned of you,' he told her softly, at last. 'But I've got news for you, Poppy. As an innocent and appallingly inexperienced virgin you might just... *just* have been able to get away with such outdated and sexually stereotyped behaviour, but since you can't any longer lay claim to your mummified virginal state it's time you learned that physical violence from a woman to a man can do a lot more than just get his adrenalin pumping... and that, in the language of sex, it can be a big come-on, as much an indication of desire as verbally saying to a man that you want him...'

'No!' Poppy asserted. Her face felt stiff, wooden, numb, so that it was almost impossible for her lips to frame the small, vehement denial.

'Yes,' James insisted softly. 'Oh, yes, Poppy—and before you start making any more denials you might also think about this. Even in the days when it was acceptable for a woman to slap a man's face, it was a weapon she used knowing that it was a two-edged sword—that the man in question might take it as the rebuke she intended but that he might retaliate by assuaging the blow to his pride by inflicting one to hers...'

When he saw the way she was looking at him, James's mouth twisted contemptuously. 'Oh, come on, Poppy,' he derided her. 'Don't tell me you've never read a book or seen a film where the hero retaliates to the heroine's slap by taking hold of her and kissing the breath out of her...'

'That's just fiction,' Poppy protested shakily. 'And besides, you... you aren't a hero... and...'

'And you certainly aren't a heroine?' James supplied for her. 'Maybe you're not, but just try remembering, the next time you feel like venting that nasty temper of yours on me, that I'm fully capable of retaliating and that I know just how to make you wish to hell that you'd had second thoughts...'

'By kissing me!' Poppy scorned, outwardly defiant but inwardly shaking with the tension and shock of the intense anger she could feel emanating from him. There had been anger between them before, but never anything like this, never anything as dangerous or out of control as the heaviness in the air she could feel vibrating between them now.

'No,' James told her quietly, shaking his head. But just as the breath was starting to leak in luxurious relief from her lungs he threw her into an ice-cold yet furnace-hot seizure of sick disbelief as he told her slowly and with obvious relish, 'No, Poppy, not by kissing you but by taking you upstairs and spreading you out beneath me on the bed and—'

'What?' Poppy dared to demand hoarsely as she tried to mask her fear. 'By raping me?'

The smile he gave her made a violent spasm of tension engulf her body, visibly shaking it whilst he watched her knowingly.

'Oh, no,' he told her silkily, 'it wouldn't be rape, Poppy, not with you crying out to me that you wanted me, begging me to touch you, to take you, to...'

She was going to faint, Poppy decided. She could already feel the coldness invading her body.

Closing her eyes, she willed the betraying symptoms to subside and not to shame her even more than she had already been shamed.

'I hate you, James,' she told her cousin through gritted teeth. 'I hate you more than I have ever hated anyone else in my life...'

She was desperately tempted to turn and walk away from him, to lose herself in the crowd. It would be easy to do... easy to escape him... but for how long? Ultimately she would have to face him and, with him, the additional taunt not just of what had happened last night but of her lack of professionalism in her work as well.

No, the best way to treat him was to behave with indifference, simply to ignore him, to distance herself completely from him and from what had happened. To close off within her mind the entire episode, to seal it up and bury it somewhere where she would never, ever have to look at it again.

'And so how are you enjoying the conference?'

Poppy made a wry face as Gunther smiled at her across the dinner table.

'I too am feeling the same,' he told her ruefully, 'and wondering if I am really in the right job. At university I had plans, dreams of being a writer, but in Germany these days it is not so easy to find a good job. My parents—my father—urged me to think of the future...' He gave a small shrug and Poppy another smile.

'But it is boring of me to talk of myself... I wish to learn more about you.'

'There isn't very much to learn,' Poppy confessed, whilst her conscience prodded her, reminding her that there was a good deal more to know than there had been twenty-four hours ago, even if it was not exactly the kind of knowledge she could ever envisage herself passing on to anyone—sharing with anyone.

It was fortunate that the Japanese businessmen whom James was dining with this evening had their own interpreter with them, even if it had galled Poppy slightly to see the way that James had watched the diminutive and very attractive Japanese woman and listened to her as she'd translated his comments to her colleagues.

He patently had a good deal more respect for her and her professional skills than he did for her own, Poppy reflected, and that knowledge rankled.

'You are looking angry,' Gunther told her. 'Have I...?'

'I was thinking about something else—someone else,' Poppy admitted.

'It is a pity that there has been so much confusion and lack of organisation over the conference,' he commented.

'Mmm,' Poppy agreed. 'Although I doubt that we would have had much time to enjoy the hotel's facilities even if they had been finished.'

'This is true,' said Gunther, and then added hesitantly, 'I had thought of hiring a car and exploring a little of the region tomorrow; I was wondering if you would care to join me...?'

Poppy was sorely tempted to agree, just for the relief of getting away from James, but, despite what James seemed to think, she did take her work seriously and she knew that if she had been here with Chris or, indeed, with any other members of the company's sales team she would never even have considered using Gunther as a means of escaping from them, and so she shook her head, gently refusing his invitation.

'Remember, if you should change your mind about joining me on my tour of the region,' Gunther told her later in the evening when they had finished their dinner, 'you only have to say.'

'You're very kind,' Poppy told him truthfully.

They had lingered in the dining room longer than most of the other diners, but Poppy was nervously aware that she couldn't put off saying goodnight to Gunther and returning to her room for much longer.

His room was in a different part of the building from hers and when they parted in the foyer Poppy felt her heart start to thud in anxious dread. Would James be in the room already? And if he was...?

By the time she had reached their floor, her hands were shaking so much that she could hardly insert the pass-card into the lock, but to her relief, when the door swung open and she stepped inside the room, there was no sign of James.

She undressed and showered quickly, unable to bring herself to look properly at her body, so that she didn't have to see those small but oh, so betraying tell-tale marks.

Once dried and wrapped in her robe she stood for several minutes on the threshold of the bedroom, staring at the pristine smoothness of the large bed, her heart pounding so heavily and painfully that she automatically put one hand over it to ease the pain it was causing her.

She couldn't sleep in that bed again, she acknowledged, licking her dry lips. She simply couldn't.

Her legs trembled as she walked quickly towards it, her glance drawn repeatedly to the door as she pulled frantically at the heavy duvet, dragging it off the bed and onto the floor, her body drenched in nervous perspiration as she prayed that James wouldn't come in before she had finished.

Even doubled over underneath her, the quilt wasn't thick enough to mask fully the hardness of the marble floor, but at least this way she was signalling unequivocally and loudly to James that, despite his goading remarks, she had no desire to endure a repetition of the previous night's events.

But as she lay tensely in the darkness Poppy knew that not all of his cruel taunts could be rejected. She *had* begged him to make love to her, she *had* responded to him, wanted him . . . she *had* been the one to insist, to demand that what was happening between them be brought to its ultimate conclusion.

'Because I wanted him to be Chris,' she whispered painfully to herself. 'I needed him to be Chris . . .'

But she had known that he wasn't. She had known that he was James—had known and had not stopped, had not ceased wanting . . . needing . . . aching . . .

The tears that burned the backs of her eyes felt like acid, raw and painful, bringing her no real relief, but then what relief could there be from the thoughts, the emotions that tormented *her*? she acknowledged miserably.

It might be impossible for her to deny or escape the taunts that James had thrown at her but it was

equally impossible for her to understand why it had
happened, why she had turned to James, responded
to James, wanted James to such an extent that she
had knowingly, wantonly and, yes, deliberately en-
couraged him to...

To what? she asked herself as the tears rolled down
her face. To have sex with her, to make love to her,
to transport her to a place she had not previously
known existed; to take her there, and once there to...?

No, no, no, Poppy denied, rolling herself even more
tightly in her duvet as she tried to stem both her tears
and the hot, raw ache burning inside her.

It was close to dawn when Poppy woke up, her body
stiff and aching, one of the pillows she had wrenched
from the bed still beneath her head, the other... Hot
scarlet colour flooded her skin betrayingly as she
realised that she had her arms wrapped round the
pillow as though...

Quickly she thrust it away from her, at the same
time lifting her head to look anxiously towards the
bed, praying that James was asleep and that he hadn't
seen the pathetic way she had cuddled up to the pillow,
her tension changing to surprise and then bewilderment as she realised that the bed was completely
empty and that James wasn't there.

If he hadn't returned to their room then where had
he spent the night—where was he spending the night?
Poppy wondered, for some reason instantly picturing
the pretty Japanese woman and the way her silvery
laughter had caused James to smile in a way he had
never smiled at her.

Had they spent the night together? Neither of them
had made any effort to conceal the fact that they found

one another attractive, Poppy acknowledged sourly. She hadn't missed the subtle message in the way that she had gently touched James's arm to underline some comment she had been making, and she certainly hadn't misinterpreted the sudden gleam in James's eyes as he'd looked back at her, nor the way in which he had moved closer to her.

Well, *she* was welcome to him, Poppy told herself fiercely. All she herself wished was that she had known what he was going to do. That way, she could have slept on the bed instead of on the floor and, instead of waking up with her body aching and her neck stiff, she would have enjoyed a decent night's sleep.

Yes, the Japanese woman was welcome to James. Poppy gave a small shudder. Did he make a habit of sleeping with two different women on consecutive nights? It seemed so out of character; she would have thought that he would have more concern for his health, more...more self-control, she decided bitterly.

It gave her a very odd and very unwanted feeling inside to think of James with another woman. Odd because that specific feeling was one she was more used to feeling in relation to Chris, and unwanted because... because...

Of course it wasn't jealousy she was feeling, Poppy comforted herself as she dragged her aching body onto the bed, hauling the duvet with her. How could it be...? She was just thankful that James wasn't here with her.

And yet, as she closed her eyes and tried to go back to sleep, no matter how hard she tried to summon up the comforting mental image of Chris's beloved features, it was James she kept on visualising. James, his eyes darkening as he leant over her.

'No,' Poppy denied aloud in growing panic. 'No, no, no...'

CHAPTER FIVE

'AH, JAMES. I am glad to see you again. It was good last night, wasn't it?'

Poppy tried not to gape as the Japanese translator came over to their stand where James had just been informing Poppy that he had some documents he wanted her to translate; the woman's eyes were eloquent with feminine emotion as she reached out and touched James's hand.

She might just as well not have been there, Poppy decided as she saw the way James turned towards the other woman, the way he smiled at her and bent his head protectively towards her.

Poppy had been midway through her breakfast when James had slid into his seat opposite her, calmly ordering his coffee without giving her any explanation of his overnight absence.

'Very good,' Poppy heard James agreeing throatily now.

Poppy could have sworn that his glance rested just a fraction too long on the other woman's body as she smiled coquettishly at him then announced that she must return to her colleagues—but not before she had leant forward and murmured provocatively to James, 'I have some free time this afternoon; you did mention that you have a car...'

Poppy waited, expecting to hear James declare in the curt way she was familiar with that he was too busy to take any time off, but, to her indignation, instead she heard him responding, 'I do indeed. What time exactly will you be free?'

As soon as the woman was out of earshot, Poppy couldn't resist reminding him, 'I thought you said we had come here to work; in fact I—'

'What's wrong?' James interrupted her, not allowing her to finish. 'Not jealous, are you?'

'Why should I be? She's welcome to you. I suppose you were with her last night, were you?'

'And if I was,' James countered urbanely, 'is that really any business of yours?'

For some reason that she could not quite define, Poppy found his relaxed and indeed almost amused attitude not only infuriating but humiliating as well.

'Yes, as a matter of fact, it is,' she told him furiously. '*You* may think nothing of going from bed to bed, woman to woman, of being... I suppose you might even have quite a high opinion of yourself for being some sort of sexual stud...' she added for good measure. 'But I am not promiscuous and I have my health to think about and—'

'Oh, do you indeed?' James interrupted her with ominous calm. 'Odd that I didn't get the impression that your health was one of your primary concerns the other night,' he goaded her bitingly.

Poppy shot him a bright-eyed look of defiant fury.

'That was because—' She started to defend herself, but James would not let her finish.

'Because you wanted to pretend I was Chris,' he finished for her, knowing well by now the way her answer would come out. 'Well, I have news for you, Poppy. When it comes down to it, far from being the untarnished, fantasy figure you seem to think he is, of the two of us I suspect that Chris would toll up

the greater number if we had to list our previous bed-
mates. So, in reality, the chances of you endangering
your "health", as you so coyly put it, would be rather
greater with him than with me.'

Poppy told him hotly, 'I don't believe what you're
saying. Chris has never...he would never... He's not
like you,' she told him flatly. 'He would never sleep
with someone just for...just for sex.'

'I never suggested that he might,' James corrected
her. 'I simply said that of the two of us he has
probably had the greater number of partners, and for
your information, Poppy, I do not sleep with women
"just for sex"...'

The look in his eyes warned Poppy not to try to
take the argument any further, but she was too wound
up, too angry to pay it any attention.

'You did with me,' she pointed out recklessly.

For a moment she thought she had won and that
he wasn't going to reply. After all, what was there
that he could honestly say?

She soon found out.

'I...had...sex...with...you,' he told her with
cold emphasis, carefully spacing out each word, so
that there was no way she could avoid their impact—
like so many carefully aimed and deliberately fired
bullets, she decided as she tried sickly to absorb their
spreading pain—'because you wouldn't let me do
anything else...'

'You're just saying that to...to punish me,' Poppy
protested, her mouth trembling as she tried to blink
away her shamed tears.

'No, Poppy, I am not,' James denied grimly. 'There
comes a point where a man—any man—simply cannot
stop. That's a known fact and I can hardly deny it,

but way before *I* had reached that point you were the
one who was ... You were the one who wanted—'

'Not you,' Poppy cut in swiftly. 'I didn't want you.
I could *never* want you.' She moved away from the
stand abruptly—so abruptly that for a moment the
hall spun dizzily around her—refusing to listen to
James as he told her to come and sit down, turning
on her heel and hurrying, almost running away from
him.

How dared he say those things to her, make her feel
so cheap, when he knew...? Well, let him go and
spend all day with his new Japanese woman-friend;
let him spend all night with her as well ... She only
wished he would.

'Poppy, what is it? What's wrong?'

As Poppy looked up into the kind, concerned face
of Gunther, she came to a sudden decision.

'Gunther,' she told him quickly, 'if that offer you
made of showing me something of the region is still
on, I've changed my mind. I would like to come with
you ...'

'It will be my pleasure,' he told her with a beaming
smile. 'I will not be free until two o'clock, though ...'

'That will be fine,' Poppy assured him. She should
have James's translations done by then so at least he
wouldn't be able to accuse her of not doing her job.
He could not accuse her of anything, she decided
fiercely, ignoring the tiny inner voice that warned her
that what she was doing was not just extremely
dangerous but potentially very irresponsible as well.

If James could take time off to enjoy himself with
his new Japanese friend, then he was hardly in a position to take her to task for doing something similar,
was he? And as for the fact that she would officially

be on company time, she would make up the hours she spent with Gunther somehow or other, she told herself grimly; that was one accusation at least that she would make sure James could not throw at her.

It was almost twelve o'clock when James came into the bedroom, where Poppy was hard at work on the translations which had proved more complex than she had originally thought. He demanded peremptorily, 'Have you finished yet, Poppy?'

'Almost,' she told him, mentally crossing her fingers that when she gave the documents a final read through she wouldn't come across anything she had missed. She didn't miss the way James's frown deepened as he looked over her shoulder at what she was doing, and she immediately challenged him defensively, 'If you're not satisfied, James, or if you think that you could have done any better...'

'If I could, the company wouldn't be employing you as a translator,' James told her crisply, picking up the work she had completed, adding as he started to read it, 'You know, Poppy, there has to be a division between our role as cousins and that of employer and employee. You're very fond of insisting that you got your job with the company on merit and not by trading on your relationship with your mother, but you don't seem to mind trading on our cousinship in our roles of employer and employee...'

'You're the one who's doing that, not me,' Poppy defended herself immediately. 'After all, if we weren't cousins, there's no way you'd have been able to force me to share a bedroom with you...'

She could see from his expression that he didn't like what she was saying. Well, tough, she decided.

He was the one who had brought the subject up, not her.

'You know your problem, don't you, James?' she challenged, swinging round to glower at him. 'You're a control freak, but you can't control *me*. No one controls me...'

'No,' James agreed drily. 'No one does, not even you.'

As he looked at her Poppy had a vivid memory of the most recent occasion on which she had betrayed her lack of self-control, and as she felt the hot tide of colour start to flood up in a give-away rush under her skin she turned quickly away from him.

'I thought you were supposed to be taking your Japanese friend out today,' she muttered as she gathered her papers together.

'I am,' James agreed, glancing at his watch as he took the papers from her. 'Have you finished now? Is everything here?'

'Yes,' Poppy confirmed tersely, noting that he was eager to be away.

'More wine?'

Poppy smiled as she shook her head, covering her almost empty glass with her hand.

'No, I suppose I hadn't better either,' Gunther agreed regretfully. 'Not as I'm driving.'

They had driven through the warm Italian countryside for almost two hours before finally stopping in a small, dusty town so pretty that it might have come straight out of a film or operetta.

They had explored it like two schoolchildren set free from their lessons, buying and eating delicious home-made ice cream the taste of which had made Poppy close her eyes in disbelieving bliss.

It had been Gunther's suggestion that, instead of heading straight back, they equip themselves with food and wine and have an impromptu picnic on the banks of the river they had seen earlier.

'Have we got time?' Poppy had asked him doubtfully. She wasn't wearing her watch and she hadn't been sure how long they had spent wandering around the town.

'We'll make time,' Gunther had told her grandly, and because she was enjoying the relaxation of being away from James and of putting to one side all the anger and anxiety that her constant confrontations with him were causing her Poppy had laughingly given in and agreed.

She had no idea now how long they had lingered over their alfresco meal, but she guessed from the lengthening shadows that it was growing late.

'We really ought to go,' she told Gunther reluctantly.

'What if I refuse?' Gunther teased her. 'What if I say that I want to keep you here for ever and never take you back?'

Even whilst she laughed, Poppy was unable to stop the sadness shadowing her eyes.

Their afternoon had given her a brief respite, but she knew that there was no real escape from her unhappiness, especially not with someone like Gunther, who, nice though he was, was no match for a man like James...

James... Poppy froze. Why should she be connecting her inability to respond to the more intimate overtures that she knew Gunther wanted to make to

James? Surely it was her love for Chris that stood between her and any other man who might show an interest in her?

'Poppy, what is it?' Gunther asked her hesitantly. 'You look so...so sad... If you have a worry...a problem...if there is something I can do to help...'

'No. It's... There is nothing...' Poppy denied quickly.

What would Gunther say, what would he think if he knew the truth? What would he think of her then? What would her friends, her family...Chris...think of her, if they knew what had happened with James...? But they would never know, she comforted herself. No one must ever know.

As she stood up and helped Gunther to clear away the remnants of their picnic, anxiety like so many sharp knives caused her darting, stabbing flickers of pain that seemed to pierce her heart and she was filled with a sense of shame, bewilderment and confusion. How could she have been like that with James...wanted him, urged him? Her hands were trembling as she picked up her jacket.

If only there were some way she could wipe the events of that night from her memory and her conscience...from hers and from James's.

It *was* late, Poppy realised once they were back in the car and heading back to the hotel. Later than she had thought, and already growing dark.

It was just as well that she had already eaten, she decided as she glanced at the clock on the car's dashboard, because they were certainly going to be too late to have dinner.

In the end it was gone ten o'clock before Gunther finally pulled into the hotel car park; a wrong turning had added several extra miles and almost a full hour to their return journey and Poppy just hoped that James was too preoccupied with his Japanese lady-friend to be aware that she had been playing truant.

'Thank you, it's been a lovely afternoon,' she told Gunther quickly, pulling away from him as he made to put his arm around her.

She could see the disappointment in his eyes but to her relief he didn't try to force the issue, simply falling into step beside her as he escorted her inside the hotel.

Once inside the foyer, Poppy searched it anxiously, but fortunately there was no sign of James.

'I'm afraid my wrong turning has caused you to miss dinner,' Gunther apologised, 'but perhaps—'

'It's all right, Gunther,' Poppy assured him, forestalling him. 'I couldn't really eat anything else anyway, not after that delicious picnic...'

If she went straight up to the room now, showered and prepared for bed, she could, with luck, be fast asleep before James came in—if indeed he was planning to spend the night with her and not with...

With her? Poppy could feel the angry, self-betraying heat burning her skin as she hurried, head defensively down, towards the lifts. Of course, she had not meant that James would be spending the night *with* her, merely that he would be spending it in their room. What had he done to her, she wondered resentfully, that she was now having to monitor even her own private thoughts?

She walked out of the lift and along the corridor, inserted her pass-card into the lock and pushed open the door.

'Where the hell have you been?'

The shock of James's unexpected presence in the bedroom caused Poppy to stare at him in speechless silence.

'Where have you been, Poppy?' he repeated.

'I...I... Out,' Poppy told him unsteadily, alarmed by his fury.

'Out. Out where?' James demanded.

'I... Gunther... I went out with Gunther,' she admitted huskily. 'He...he had hired a car for the afternoon and he wanted—'

'Spare me the details, I can well imagine exactly what it was he wanted,' James told her savagely. 'And, to judge from the look of you and the length of time you've been gone, he got it.

'Did you enjoy it, Poppy?' he demanded acidly. 'Did you beg him...plead with him—?'

Before she knew what she was doing Poppy had flown at James, raising her hand to bring it down hard against his face, goaded beyond endurance by the hateful things he was saying to her, desperate to make him stop.

But instead of retreating from her, instead of reacting as she had imagined and recognising how offensive, how unbearable, how unwarranted and undeserved his accusations were, he took hold of her with such speed that she had no time to do anything other than give a small gasp of startled shock as his fingers manacled her wrists and he swung her round in front of him, using his weight and her vulnerability to tip her over onto the bed.

As he leaned over her, imprisoning her, Poppy could see the dark flecks in the topaz brilliance of his eyes, which, when she focused on them, seemed to mesmerise her into a state of shocked numbness. Then

she heard him say, 'I warned you what would happen
if you did that again, Poppy.'

And then he was raising her hands above her head,
holding them, shackling them there, his body poised
powerfully over hers.

'I know why you're doing this,' Poppy protested
wildly. 'You're doing it to punish me because your
pride can't bear knowing that I don't want you.'

'Is that what you told your German friend?' James
snarled at her.

'Gunther and I just spent the afternoon together.
We didn't ... he's not ...'

Poppy tensed as she realised that her efforts to break
free of James's constraining hold had caused the soft,
full skirt she was wearing to ride up, exposing her
thighs.

'Let me go, James,' she begged shakily when she
saw the way he was looking at her body. 'You don't
really want me,' she added huskily, 'You can't,
and—'

'Who says I can't?' James taunted her softly. 'I'm
a man, Poppy, and, as any man will tell you, there's
nothing quite so erotically stimulating as having a
woman tell you she wants you, as having her beg you
to fulfil her and satisfy her, as having her cry out to
you that she needs you, aches for you ...'

'No,' Poppy denied in panic. 'I didn't mean it ...
I ... You can't do this, James. I don't want you ...'

'Liar,' he told her softly, and as though to prove
her self-deceit he reached out his free hand and ran
it slowly up over her trembling body.

The hard, warm feel of his palm against the tense
sensitivity of her bare thigh made her quiver from
head to foot in what Poppy told herself despairingly

was outrage and rejection, but long before James's hand had smoothed its way over her waist to lie mockingly just below the full curve of her breast she knew that she was lying to herself.

'But I *can't* want you...'

She hadn't realised she had whispered the shocked words out loud until she heard James warning her through gritted teeth, 'Take care I don't make you eat those words, Poppy, or endure the sexual equivalent, because, I promise you, if I do...once I do...'

Poppy's whole body shuddered as she realised what he meant, realised and, to her appalled anguish, visibly reacted to that knowledge not with shock and rejection but instead with something—some need— she couldn't bear to acknowledge.

'I don't want this, James,' she told him defiantly, but she knew as he lifted his hand and slowly started to unfasten her top that she was lying, and, what was worse, she knew that he knew it too.

Why, why was her body responding to him like this? she wondered helplessly as he peeled away her top to reveal the warm curves of her breasts.

She tried to will her body not to react to the warmth of James's breath as he bent his head towards her.

'No!'

Even as she made the thick, guttural denial and twisted her body desperately from side to side, Poppy knew shamingly that, far from making her want to be released from the sensual bondage of James's mouth's possession of her breast, the deepening and intensifying sensation of that possession as he subdued her attempts to break free of him somehow only increased the erotic effect of his mouth against her body.

Lost in the sensation caused by James's mouth slowly savaging the sensitive flesh of her breasts, Poppy was unaware of the fact that he had unfastened and removed her skirt until she felt the sudden coolness of the air-conditioning against her bare skin, her only covering the small white triangle of her cotton briefs.

James still had her hands pinned above her head, and as he released her breast and started to unfasten his shirt Poppy turned her head to avoid looking at him, knowing already what just the thought of the satin heat of his naked skin against her own was doing to her, and as she did so she inadvertently caught sight of her reflection in the mirror on the wall, her body tensing as she stared transfixed at her image, unable to withdraw her gaze.

Was that really her, that creature with the dark, tangled mane of hair, the full, swollen mouth whose colour echoed that of her erotically pouting nipples, her skin so creamily pale, so silky and glistening as she lay against the coverlet of the bed, her spine arched, her body stretched out like some wanton, sensual offering?

Even to her own eyes there was something about her almost voluptuous dishevelment, the disarrangement of her limbs that positively flaunted her sensuality, her sexuality, she recognised in wide eyed shock, the white triangle of her briefs somehow more of an enticement than a barrier, her thighs slightly parted as though ... as though ...

'What are you looking at?' she heard James ask as he pulled off his shirt and stepped out of his trousers and leaned towards her, his image joining hers in the mirror, his mouth curling in a smile that made her stomach muscles lock in protest against the wave of shocked excitement it caused her.

'Ah,' he said softly, 'so you like looking at yourself, do you, Poppy? You like watching whilst—?'

'No,' Poppy protested, her face burning as she heard him laugh and saw the way he stretched out his hand and slowly ran his fingertips along her skin, making her shiver and tremble in helpless response.

'Well, remember what I said about making you eat your words,' he reminded her softly. 'Would you like that, Poppy?' he added, so gently that the words slipped up under her guard. 'Would you like to know what it feels like to have a man's mouth against your body whilst he . . . ?'

His hand was covering her sex now, not touching or caressing her, simply lying there, but the weight and heat of it, the knowledge of it, was enough to accelerate the pulse which had been slowly throbbing there ever since he had first taken hold of her— throbbing in a deep, fierce ache so intense that she felt sure that he must be able to feel the vibrations as they shook her helpless body.

He was naked now, his body darkly powerful in contrast to hers, his skin like the taut, warm pelt of a jungle killer.

The urge within her to reach out and touch it, to touch him was so compelling that Poppy couldn't withstand it, her fingertips trembling as they finally came into contact with his body.

The fierce shudder that ripped through him made her stare at him in confused surprise, her eyes staring straight up into the dark heat of his, her breath coming faster between her half-parted lips as her body responded instinctively in its recognition of the arousal of his.

For some reason his arousal shocked her. Shocked her and excited her, she acknowledged, unaware that her eyes were betraying her emotions to him, unaware of anything other than the heat and power of him as he lowered his body against hers and took hold of her, smothering any protest she might have wanted to make.

Whilst her body shivered its pleasure in his arms, her lips responded to the pressure of his, parting, opening, her mouth drinking in the taste and feel of him.

In the distance Poppy could hear a sound—a soft, keening cry of desire and urgency that she didn't recognise as hers until James lifted his mouth from hers and demanded roughly, 'Now tell me that you don't want *me* ... that you want my brother.

'Look, Poppy,' he commanded, one hand cupping the side of her face, turning it so that she was forced to look at her reflection in the mirror—at *their* reflections in the mirror—at the way that, without knowing she had done so, she had arched herself against him, opened her thighs to accept the weight of one of his between them, to accept it and ...

Poppy shivered as she saw the way her flesh clung longingly to his, the way her whole body silently betrayed its yearning need.

'No ... No, this isn't what I want,' she protested in a panicky whisper. 'This can't be what I want. *You* aren't what I want ...'

As she tried to push James away, to reassert her independence, her determination to reject everything that both he and her body were telling her, she saw anger and another emotion she couldn't define flash like warning darts of fire through the brilliance of his eyes.

'Why are you doing this?' she protested huskily. 'You don't want me. You don't even like me. You must want... What happened?' she asked him bitterly. 'Did your Japanese lady-friend turn you down after all? Well, that's not my fault, so don't try to...to...take out your frustration on me.'

'Why not?' James challenged her brutally. 'Why shouldn't I use you the way you used me? Exactly the way you used me!'

Poppy gasped in shock at the ugliness of his accusation. 'That's not fair... It's not...it's not true,' she defended herself. 'What happened the other night was a...a mistake,' she told him shakily.

'Was it? Well, there won't be any mistakes this time,' James responded mirthlessly. 'Look into the mirror, Poppy,' he instructed her again, adding forcefully when she tried to turn her head away, 'Look...and tell me what you see.'

Poppy's whole body trembled beneath the weight of her emotions. How could she tell him what she saw? How could she shame herself by putting into words what her body was so obviously experiencing—the desire, the need...the sensuality she could see in every taut line of her flesh, every aching curve, every inch of the body she could barely recognise as her own as she was forced to look, witness its open hunger for the man holding it?

The man holding it... And that man was James. *Not* Chris but James. James, whom she could not possibly cerebrally want or desire, whom she did not even like, never mind love.

What had happened to her? she wondered helplessly as she caught back a panicky sob. And why had
it happened to her? Why had her own flesh so
blatantly turned traitor on her? Why was it...she...so
out of control, so...so...

'The other night you told me you wanted
me...begged me to make love to you. This time, when
you say those words again, there'll be no taking them
back, Poppy, no pretence that you think I am Chris.
This time both of us know just who exactly it is you're
crying out for.'

Was that why he was doing this to her? Poppy wondered achingly. Because his pride couldn't stomach
the thought that a woman—any woman, but most especially a woman whom, after all, he had made it
clear he despised so absolutely and completely—
should dare to prefer another man? Was this, then,
male pride, male anger, male desire, male power generated and fed by some testosterone-fuelled need to
be first, to be the best?

'Say it again, Poppy,' she heard James demanding
softly as his mouth started to caress her throat in what
she knew was a slow and deliberate assault on her
defences. 'Tell me you want me...'

'No,' Poppy refused stubbornly, panicked by the
thought of losing control, by the knowledge that what
he was doing could all too easily *make* her lose control.

She felt her whole body shudder as his mouth
burned paths of fire down over it. In the mirror she
could see her tortured twisting and turning as she tried
to evade his lips and hands, but already her denials
and her movements possessed a slow, drugged quality
that made them sound and look more like some subtle
form of enticement than genuine rejection.

There was something about the sight of James leaning over her, half straddling her, something about the sheer, naked power of his body that sent waves of heat blistering through her, that made the hands she knew she had reached out to fend him off somehow seek to draw him closer instead.

When she felt the warmth of his mouth caressing her stomach, she cried out to him to stop, but his hands were already sliding her briefs free of her body, and although she fought desperately not to look the sight of his dark head against the pale silkiness of her thighs caused such a fierce spasm of sensation within her that her whole body jerked visibly.

'No, don't—please don't,' she whispered protestingly, but his hands were already holding her, lifting her, his lips stroking the soft, vulnerable flesh on the inside of her thighs, his palm resting against her sex, touching it, making it...her...tremble in a paroxysm of combined anxiety and pleasure.

Even though she had known what was going to happen, *how* he was going to punish her and exact full payment for her defiance, her denial, and, even though she had thought she had prepared her body so that she could defend herself from it, the shock of his mouth actually moving against the most intimate part of her—and her reaction to it—caused her to cry out helplessly to him that she couldn't bear such pleasure, that she was afraid of what he was going to do to her, of what she was feeling.

'James... James...'

She heard herself call his name as her body exploded in violent spasms of intense pleasure and knew she was babbling incoherently to him as he moved over her and took her in his arms, kissing her breasts

and then her mouth with the taste of her body still
on his lips.

'James ... James ...'

Her body was still quivering, still empty...still
aching for him, she recognised in breathless wonder.

'Say it,' he demanded against her mouth. 'Say the
words, Poppy...'

'I want you,' she told him helplessly. 'I want you...
I want you ...'

The words became a dizzy cry reinforcing each
thrust of his body within hers—a meaningless litany
to accompany the waves of pleasure and need that
were building higher and higher.

Poppy heard herself cry out his name again as the
pleasure finally crested, her body damp and
weak...drained of life and energy as she clung to him
in the aftermath of her passion.

In the mirror she could still see their reflection, their
bodies entwined. She could feel the tears sliding helplessly down her face. What had she done...? What
had she become ...? She no longer recognised herself
in the person she now seemed to be and that made
her feel more desperately afraid than she had ever felt
in the whole of her life.

It was only as she finally slid into an exhausted sleep
that she realised that she had barely thought of Chris
since she had walked into the bedroom and seen
James.

Because she couldn't bear to think of Chris and the
purity of her love for him after what she had done—
after what James had made her do, she told herself
numbly as sleep finally claimed her.

CHAPTER SIX

'POPPY, can you come down to my office, please? There's something we need to discuss.'

Poppy could feel the palms of her hands growing clammy with nervous perspiration as she clung tightly to the telephone receiver.

'Does it have to be now, James?' she asked tersely. 'Only I'm just in the middle of working on those Japanese documents you want and—'

'Now, Poppy,' James interrupted her curtly.

As Poppy replaced the receiver she stared unseeingly through her office window, oblivious to the neat trimness of the grass borders broken up by colourful patches of shrubs which decorated the company's car park.

They had been back from Italy almost ten weeks— long enough, surely, for her to have at least begun to get over the shock of what had happened when they were there. But instead she had taken to avoiding James as much as she possibly could and suspected that he was doing exactly the same thing with her.

Pushing her chair away from her desk, she stood up, gritting her teeth against the nervous dizziness making her head swim and her heart pound with sick tension.

Unlike most heads of businesses, James preferred to have his office on the ground floor. It helped to keep his feet on the ground, he had once told Poppy sternly when she had questioned such unusual behaviour. A successful business was like a pyramid, he had added obliquely, and whoever stood at its peak was in a very vulnerable position unless he or she knew that the base on which it was constructed was stable and able to support the rest of the structure.

Then, as a teenager, Poppy hadn't truly understood what he meant; now she did and, albeit rather begrudgingly, had to respect him for it.

As she hurried down the two flights of stairs to the ground floor she wondered nervously why James wanted to see her. It couldn't be anything to do with the documents she was working on, they hadn't reached the deadline for those yet.

Walking along the corridor to James's office, she saw that the door to Chris's office was open, but, true to the vow she had made herself on the day of his and Sally's wedding, she refused to give in to the temptation to look to see if he was there.

There was no sign of James's secretary as Poppy hovered outside his closed office door. She knocked reluctantly and then went in.

James was seated behind the desk which, like all the other furniture in the room, was strictly utilitarian. He did not believe in wasting company money on non-productive luxuries, and yet, disconcertingly, the lack of normal, status-symbol fittings seemed to emphasise the aura of leadership and power that emanated from him rather than diminish it.

He was her cousin as well as her boss and it was ridiculous that she should feel like a child summoned before a disapproving teacher, Poppy decided as she waited to hear why he had sent for her.

There were some papers on the desk in front of him and her heart missed a beat as she saw the familiar letterhead of the Italian spa.

'Stewart Thomas asked to see me this morning,' he told Poppy, referring to the company's accountant.

Poppy's heart started to thump even more heavily. She had submitted her quarterly expenses to the accounts department the previous week. She was always painstakingly careful with them, but ever since James had hauled her over the coals for inadvertently putting a private petrol bill through her expenses she had lived in nervous dread of accidentally repeating her error.

'If it's about my expenses,' she began quickly, 'I—'

'No, Poppy, it's not about your expenses,' James told her. 'It's about this.' He picked up the letter in front of him as he spoke and pushed it across the desk towards her.

Uneasily Poppy picked it up.

'It's the bill from the Italian hotel,' she acknowledged. 'I . . . I understood I didn't have any expenses for that. You—'

'This isn't about your expenses, Poppy,' James repeated grimly. 'At least not in the way you mean. Take another look at the bill and this time read it properly, or would you prefer me to do it for you? Perhaps I should; that way we might at least save some time,' he told her curtly, flicking the paper away from her and reading out the words. 'Mr and Mrs Carlton: one double room.'

Poppy stared at him, the colour leaving her face, driven out as much by the acid note she could hear in his voice as by what he had actually said.

'But...but it was a mistake... They made a mistake,' she told him huskily. 'You said so yourself... You said...'

'It doesn't matter *what* I said,' James told her. 'What matters is the interpretation that Stewart Thomas and no doubt anyone else who happens to have seen this is going to put on it. The mere fact that he felt he ought to bring it straight to me says it all... don't you agree?'

Poppy felt sick.

'But you paid the bill before we left. They gave you a receipt, and—'

'And now they've sent a copy of it here,' James told her. 'God knows how many people had already seen it before it reached Stewart's desk.'

'But...but you explained to him what happened...? That the hotel had made a mistake, that they were overbooked.'

'Oh, yes, I told him,' James agreed, 'but—' He stopped speaking as his office door was unceremoniously pushed open and Chris hurried in, looking uncertain and confused.

'James, I don't know what's going on, but I've just overheard—' He broke off when he saw Poppy, looking frowningly from her stricken white face to James's grimly angry one.

'Yes, Chris, what have you overheard?' James probed.

'Well, I don't suppose it means anything, but as I walked past the general office I heard one of the girls talking about the fact that you and Poppy had...were... They're saying that the two of you are lovers,' he finished awkwardly. 'The whole place is buzzing with it,' he added. 'What on earth's going on?'

Whilst Chris had been talking James had stepped out from behind his desk and was now, Poppy realised, standing next to her.

As Chris looked at them both, to Poppy's shock James reached out and took hold of her hand, linking fingers with hers and then squeezing hers warningly as he said, 'We had hoped to keep it to ourselves for a little while longer but ... yes, it's true; Poppy and I—'

'But this is wonderful,' Chris interrupted him enthusiastically. 'Just wait until I tell Sally. When did all this happen and why haven't you said anything? Too preoccupied with other things, I suppose,' he chuckled. 'I know how it was with me and Sally when we first fell in love and I've no need to ask if you are in love, you must be, James, if you were idiotic enough to think the pair of you could get away with booking into a double room without anyone finding out. Have you told the family yet or—?'

'We didn't—' Poppy began quickly, anxious to make him understand that he had got it wrong, that there was nothing between her and James, that it was all a horrible mistake, that ...

But James stopped her, the pressure of his grip on her fingers silencing her denial in her throat, his voice overriding hers as he told Chris smoothly, 'We didn't want to say anything to anyone yet. It's all so new to us that we wanted to keep our ... feelings to ourselves.'

'Well, you can hardly do that now,' Chris laughed. 'Not with the whole place knowing that the two of you have spent four nights in bed together.'

Poppy had to bite down hard on her bottom lip to prevent herself crying out with pain as she heard the amusement in his voice. Didn't he *know*, didn't he *care* that *he* was the one she loved, not James?

'Just wait until I tell Sally,' he repeated.

Poppy burst out frantically, 'No...'

'No,' James concurred, giving Poppy's tender fingers another warning squeeze as Chris gave her a surprised look. 'Not yet. We still need a little more time to ourselves.'

'Well, you're going to have to go public with the family soon,' Chris warned him. 'They're bound to hear the gossip that's going round. I know that Ma and Aunt Fee only come in once a month or so, but—'

'Thanks, Chris,' James interrupted his brother. 'I hear what you are saying but...'

'But it isn't anything to do with me,' Chris finished cheerfully for him. 'Well, I doubt you'll get either Ma or Aunt Fee to agree with that, and you know that it's Aunt Fee's annual birthday lunch on Sunday. You're not going to find it easy to keep them from guessing the truth; after all, the family is used to seeing the pair of you either quarrelling or ignoring one another, not holding hands and...'

Immediately Poppy tried to pull her hand away but James refused to let her go.

If he wasn't going to tell Chris the truth then she would just have to, Poppy decided, turning away from James to reach out imploringly to Chris with her other hand as she began, 'Chris, please, there's—'

'Chris, that call has come through for you from Bensons,' Chris's secretary interrupted, putting her head round the door to give him the message.

'Thanks ... I'm on my way,' he responded, pausing only to say ruefully to Poppy and James, 'You might as well tell them, you know; there's no way you're going to be able to keep it a secret now ...'

Poppy could hardly contain herself long enough for Chris to close the door behind him before she turned on James and demanded furiously, 'Why didn't you tell him the truth? Why—?'

'What truth?' James interrupted her. 'Is that really what you want me to do, Poppy?' he asked curtly. 'Do you really want me to tell Chris what happened— *exactly* what happened, *everything* that happened?' he emphasised cruelly.

Humiliated, Poppy looked away from him.

'No, you know that's not what I meant,' she admitted, white-faced, adding in a choked whisper, 'But you had no need to let him think, to let him believe that ...'

'That what—that you and I are lovers? What would you have preferred me to do? Tell him it was just sex ... just a four-night stand.'

'You could have said it was a mistake,' Poppy burst out. 'You could have told him that the hotel was confused by the fact that we share the same surname ...'

'I could, yes,' James agreed. 'And then what ...?'

'What do you mean?' Poppy asked him in confusion.

'If I had told him that, Chris would have been bound to ask what had happened, how we had resolved the mistake. In other words, Poppy, he would have expected me to say that the mistake was put right and that we were given separate rooms if not separate bills.'

'And whose fault was it that we weren't?' Poppy demanded frantically. 'We can't let people think that...that we are lovers,' she told him miserably.

'We can't let people, or we can't let Chris?' James demanded. 'Face it, Poppy, he couldn't care less. In fact he's probably relieved to have you off his back. It's time you started living in the real world, Poppy. You and I—'

'There is no *you and I*,' Poppy denied fiercely. 'I hate knowing what happened between us,' she told him passionately. 'I feel sick every time I think about it. I know you've always hated and despised me, James; well, now you've made me hate and despise myself even more than you do.' She headed for his office door. 'No more, James. I just can't take any more.'

'Poppy, are you sure you're all right?'

Poppy gave her mother a lacklustre smile and fibbed, 'Yes, I'm fine.'

'She's probably missing James,' Chris teased her. He and Sally had arrived minutes earlier, the first guests to arrive for her mother's annual birthday lunch, and the four of them were standing in her parents' conservatory whilst her father poured the drinks.

Poppy shot her mother an anxious look, but she appeared to have missed Chris's comment.

'Don't worry, he'll be here,' Chris told Poppy. 'He rang me last night to say he'd be bringing Ma with him.'

For the first time since she had fallen in love with him Poppy found that she actively didn't want to be with Chris. She could tell from the looks he and Sally were exchanging that he *had* told his wife about her supposed relationship with James.

How many of the other guests her mother had invited also knew about it? Poppy wondered, her face burning. Where *was* James? What was she going to do if he didn't arrive...if she was left to face people's questions and curiosity on her own? A dizzy panicky feeling gripped her as she looked anxiously through the drawing-room window, searching for some sign of James's arrival.

'Poppy, what is it? Who are you looking for?' her mother asked her.

'N-nothing...no one,' Poppy stammered, but she knew that her face was flushing guiltily and she could see that her mother was puzzled by her behaviour.

'Poppy, my dear...and how was Italy?' a friend and neighbour of her parents enquired heartily after he'd greeted her mother. 'A beautiful country and, of course, you went with James who is part-Italian himself...'

'Oh, have you and James been on holiday together?' a slightly deaf great-aunt asked with interest, picking up on the conversation. 'How nice; I always thought that the two of you would be well suited.'

'James and Poppy went away together to Italy on business,' Poppy's mother explained hastily.

Nearly all the guests had arrived now and Poppy's heart missed a beat as she saw Stewart Thomas and his wife on the opposite side of the room. She had had no idea that her mother had asked him and his wife to come. What was she going to do if Stewart said something to her mother about the hotel bill?

Panic seized her. Had James done this deliberately—left her on her own to face the consequences of what she had done? She started to shiver as her panic turned to a cold sweat of sick fear. How was she going to face everyone—her parents, her family?

James had to come, she reassured herself. He was bringing his mother. Chris had told her so. She could see Stewart Thomas and his wife talking together and she was sure that she was the subject of their discussion from the way they kept looking across at her.

A car drew up outside and James and Chris's mother got out, but James wasn't with her, Poppy realised in dismay as she recognised her aunt's companion as a long-standing male friend.

'Oh, dear, are we the last to arrive?' Poppy heard her aunt saying as her parents welcomed them in. 'I'm so sorry. There was a last-minute change of plan; James was supposed to be bringing us.'

'Don't worry, it's a cold lunch,' Poppy's mother responded. 'Come in and have a drink.'

Why wasn't her mother asking where James was? Poppy worried frantically. Why hadn't her aunt *said* why he wasn't with them?

'Poppy, you're looking awfully pale; I hope that son of mine isn't working you too hard. How was Italy, by the way? The countryside in that area is just so magnificent. I haven't seen you since you got back...'

Poppy glanced nervously over her shoulder before responding to her. Stewart was standing within earshot of their conversation, talking now to her own father.

'I...'

'Oh, I don't think Poppy got an awful lot of time to look at the scenery,' Chris informed his mother, giving Poppy a wicked look. 'Although I do believe she has become a devout admirer of a certain aspect of Italian—'

'James!'

Poppy couldn't contain her relief as she saw the tall, familiar figure striding into the room. The agonised, reproachful look she had been about to give Chris was forgotten as she hurried across to James's side, her brain not registering the surprise on some people's faces and the more worrying knowledge and amusement on others' until it was too late—until she had reached James's side, until she had clutched anxiously at his arm, until she had by her own actions and in full view of everyone there confirmed all that she had told James so fiercely *he* had to deny.

'Poppy?' she heard her mother saying uncertainly, her face registering her disbelief that Poppy should even acknowledge James's presence, never mind rush across the room to virtually throw herself into his arms, to clutch at him as though he were her only life raft in a life-threatening sea.

'You'll have to tell them now,' Poppy heard Chris chuckling. He and Sally, as well as her own father and mother and aunt, had followed her to James's side and all were now looking at them.

'Tell us what?' Poppy's mother asked, puzzled.

Helplessly Poppy looked at James.

'Poppy and I—' James began quietly.

But Chris beat him to it, informing them happily, 'Poppy and James are in love; in fact—'

'At last. Oh, Poppy I can't tell you how happy this makes me!' her aunt exclaimed. 'The two of you have always been so right for one another. I can still remember the way you used to follow James around when you were a child. Virtually as soon as you could walk you used to toddle after him, and now—'

'And now she's finally caught up with him,' Chris teased, interrupting his mother who was dabbing the emotional tears from her eyes as she hugged Poppy.

'How long have you known?'

'When did all this happen?'

'Have you made any plans yet?'

Poppy stood like someone in a trance as her family's happy congratulations fell on her like blows, whilst at her side James was as still and cold as stone.

'I told you you'd never be able to keep this to yourselves,' Chris reminded them gleefully when Poppy's father had gone to open some champagne.

'*Now* I know why you looked so disappointed when I arrived without James.' James's mother smiled as she hugged Poppy a second time. 'Oh, Poppy, I can't tell you how pleased I am... I thought that James—' She broke off and shook her head, smiling at Poppy through her tears.

What was wrong with them all? Poppy wondered dizzily as her father started to hand round glasses of champagne. They all knew that she loved Chris and yet they were behaving as though... as though her relationship with James was somehow expected... a foregone conclusion.

She heard her father proposing a toast whilst someone else congratulated James and asked him when they were to be married.

'Well, you won't want to wait long, will you?' interrupted Sally. 'And, after all, it isn't as though you need to look for a house or anything; you can move straight into James's...'

Could she see just the tiniest hint of relief in Sally's eyes? Poppy wondered achingly as Chris turned to hug her. He didn't kiss her, she noticed. Did he suspect the truth...? Did he know that *he* was still the one she loved?

'So when did all this happen?' Poppy's mother asked her when the excitement had finally started to die down a little.

In Italy, Poppy was about to say, but James got in before her, saying firmly, 'Last Christmas.'

Poppy turned her head to stare at him. Last Christmas they had had one of the worst quarrels they had ever had, when he'd accused her of trying to make Sally uncomfortable at the family's Christmas party by 'mooning about', as he'd put it, over Chris.

She waited for her mother to laugh and accuse James of lying but instead she simply smiled and said that they had done very well to keep it to themselves for so long.

'We didn't want to steal Chris and Sally's glory,' James fibbed smoothly.

'So now we've got another wedding to plan; when do you...?'

A wedding... Poppy gave James an appalled look and told her mother quickly, 'Oh, no, we can't—'

'We can't quite make up our minds when,' James overrode her smoothly.

'Well, at least you won't have to look for a house,' her mother continued, repeating what Sally had said earlier, giving James a rueful look as she added, 'I thought at the time that it was rather odd for a single man to be buying what was obviously a family home. I suppose I should have guessed then; Poppy has always had a weakness for those Victorian houses down by the river.'

Whilst Poppy bit back her shocked response—that she had had nothing to do with the choice of James's present home—James himself responded with a calm, 'Yes, I know; I remember how as a little girl she used to insist on taking the long way home from school so that she could walk past them.'

It was true, she *did* love the magnificent terrace of large Victorian houses whose long gardens backed onto the river, and had even fantasised about living in one, but with Chris, not James.

She had been angry when James had bought one of them, resentful almost, refusing to go to the small house-warming party he had given.

All through lunch Poppy was conscious of the interest they were causing. She herself didn't have any appetite, she had lost weight since her return from Italy but then she was so stressed, so on edge that it was no wonder she didn't want to eat.

'I want to talk to you.' Poppy tensed as she heard James speaking quietly in her ear.

'We can't... not now. Not here.'

'I'm leaving in half an hour,' James told her, glancing at his watch, 'and when I do you're coming with me.'

'No,' Poppy protested. 'I can't... What will people think?'

'They'll think that we're in love and that we want to be on our own to—'

'Stop it,' Poppy hissed, her face starting to burn. 'Why did you have to say... to let them think...?'

'Why the hell do you think?' James demanded grimly.

Poppy's flush deepened as she remembered that all too betraying 'James!' and the way she had virtually flung herself into his arms.

'Where are we going?' Poppy asked James after she had fastened her seat belt. She had tried to get out of leaving with him, using the excuse that her mother would need her to help clear up, but James had refused to listen and now here she was, seated next to him in his car, wondering why on earth she had been so stupid as to allow the curious glances of a few people to drive her into seeing James as an ally...a refuge.

'Where do you think?' James asked her drily as he turned the car in the direction of his own home.

'Not there,' Poppy protested as she realised where they were going.

'Why not? Where else is there where we can talk without being overheard?'

'We don't have to go to your house. You could just park the car and...say...'

'Oh, yes, and have anyone who saw us—and certainly someone would—put it about that the pair of us are so hot for each other that you'll let me have you in the back of the car?'

'Stop it,' Poppy demanded, hot-cheeked. 'Don't talk about me like that. I would never...' She stopped, the words of denial choking in her throat. How could she tell James that what he was saying made her feel cheap? It was too late to argue with him any more. He was already turning into the road to his house, which was right at the end of the terrace and had a large expanse of garden to the side of it as well as to the rear.

The houses, three storeys high, possessed cellars as well as attics, most of which had been converted into garages and storage spaces respectively. As James parked his car in his garage, she shivered a little, dreading the interview ahead.

'This way,' James instructed her, opening the car door for her.

As she followed him up stone steps and through a door into the main hallway she tried not to betray any interest in the house which she had so far refused to visit, even though her eye was immediately taken by the elegance of the plasterwork ceiling and the generous proportions of the hall and stairs.

The rich mahogany of the panelled doors gleamed softly in the early evening sunlight and Poppy had to suppress an urge to reach out and touch them to see if the wood felt as warmly alive as it looked. Disconcertingly, she remembered that the last time she had felt such an urge to touch something that something had been James—the sleek warmth of James's body.

A fierce shudder galvanised her body, causing James to frown as he watched her. The stairs and hallway had been carpeted in a natural cord matting which provided the perfect background for the richness of the rugs laid over it. If this had been her home she would have added some feminine touches such as a huge bowl of flowers on the circular table, Poppy decided, but otherwise she couldn't fault James's taste.

'In here,' he told her, opening one of the doors.

Poppy blinked as she stepped through it and was momentarily blinded by sunlight. The room was huge, running the whole length and half the width of the ground floor, with windows overlooking both the front and the back, and James had furnished it with a mixture of antique and modern furniture which somehow melded magically together to make it look both elegant and welcoming.

'Now,' James began as he followed her into the room and closed the door behind him, 'do you mind telling me exactly what you're playing at?'

'I . . . I don't know what you mean,' Poppy said.

'Oh, come on, Poppy, don't give me that. What the hell were you doing coming up to me like that and making it obvious that—?'

'That what?' Poppy defended herself, tears stinging her eyes. 'That we'd been to bed together? They already knew that—or they would soon have known,' she amended more honestly.

James was frowning. 'What do you mean? Surely Chris—?'

'Not Chris,' Poppy interrupted. 'No one had said anything, but Mum had invited Stewart Thomas and I could tell from the way he and Diana were looking at me . . .' She bit her lip, unwilling to tell him how vulnerable she had felt, how afraid and alone it had made her realise she was when she had seen the way Stewart and his wife were looking at her and had known what they must be saying.

'It's all right for you,' she told James fiercely. 'No one would think any the less of you for . . . for what happened . . . but it's different for me.

'Why did all this have to happen?' she demanded passionately, tears clogging her voice.

'Do you *really* have to ask?' she heard James saying roughly. 'It had to happen because of this, Poppy. Because of this . . .' And then he was holding her, kissing her, his mouth almost brutal as it devoured hers, but even more shocking than the raw sensuality of his kiss was her own response to it—her *body's* response to it: avid, eager, hungry, shamelessly accepting, urging, inciting him to...

Poppy gave a small moan of panic as she felt his hand move towards her breast. Once he touched her there she would have no hope of stopping the frightening, out-of-control rush of sensation that she could feel building inside her, threatening her. As she panicked and started to pull away from James, she was engulfed by the return of the dizzy sensation she had felt earlier on, only this time it was accompanied by a surge of nausea and weakness.

Helpless to escape it, she closed her eyes and gave a small moan.

'Poppy—Poppy, what is it?' she heard James demanding forcefully as she fell forward against him. When his arms locked round her to support her, she felt the dizziness start to recede and, mercifully, with it her nausea.

'How long has this been going on?' James asked her curtly. He was still holding her, still supporting her, and inexplicably it was somehow easier simply to stay where she was, leaning against him, than to make herself move away; her legs still felt oddly weak and she couldn't get out of her mind how afraid and vulnerable she had felt when he hadn't been there, how relieved she had been to see him standing there in her parents' drawing room.

'How long has *what* been going on?' she asked him weakly.

'You know what I mean, Poppy,' James warned her harshly. 'Are you pregnant? Are you carrying my child?' he asked her grimly.

Carrying his child. The colour came and went in Poppy's face as the importance of what he was saying struck her.

'No, no, of course I'm not,' she denied. How...? 'I can't be pregnant, James,' she told him piteously. 'I can't be...'

'You may not *want* to be,' James corrected her bitingly.

Pregnant, with James's child... Poppy swayed shakily. Of course she couldn't be...could she? As she mentally counted the weeks and then slowly recounted them since their return from Italy and acknowledged what she had previously ignored—namely that her period was now months overdue—she went cold with shock.

'Poppy?' James demanded gratingly.

'I...I don't know,' she whispered through numb lips, and then as the panic exploded inside her she told him frantically, 'James, I can't be pregnant... We can't...'

'It's perhaps just as well that we've already warned everyone that we intend to get married,' James told her curtly, ignoring her shocked denial and coolly interpreting the reason for her panic.

'We can't get married,' Poppy protested, her eyes glazed with shock.

'We can't not,' James corrected her. 'Not now.'

'But I may *not* be pregnant,' Poppy told him. 'And even if I am...'

'If you are, what?' James asked her harshly. 'If you are, you'd rather destroy my child than—?'

'No,' Poppy told him vehemently. 'No, I could never do that...never.'

'Then we don't really have any other option, do we?' James told her. 'If you *are* carrying my child, we *have* to get married...'

'Yes,' Poppy whispered, knowing that it was true. Had they been strangers and not cousins maybe then she could have contemplated bringing her child up alone, but under the circumstances...

'I may not be pregnant,' she repeated, but she could hear the lack of conviction in her voice and knew that James could hear it too.

As she closed her eyes she had a vivid memory of feeling James deep within her body, of experiencing that fierce, female surge of triumph at knowing that he was there, without realising then just what that feeling meant. Now she suspected that she did. She'd have to get one of those test things from the chemist's, she decided bleakly; either that or visit their family doctor.

'I never wanted this to happen,' she told James bleakly. 'I never wanted—'

'Either me or my child?' he suggested. 'No, I know that...I...No doubt you'd far rather fantasise that it's Chris's child you're carrying, just as you wanted to fantasise that he was the one making love to you. Unfortunately—for both of us—it wasn't him. It was me!'

CHAPTER SEVEN

'POPPY, I need to talk to you.' Poppy shivered as she listened to the curt tones of James's voice relaying the terse message to her over her answering machine.

Mercifully, at least as far as she was concerned, he had been away on business for the past three days and today she wasn't going into the office since she was taking three days' holiday. Later in the day she was due to have lunch with Sally's stepmother and her fellow bridesmaid—an arrangement which had been made at Star's suggestion three months ago, on the day of Chris and Sally's wedding.

As she remembered the certainty and vehemence with which she had insisted then that there was no way she would ever marry, Poppy could feel her stomach starting to churn nauseously with a now familiar mixture of panic and misery.

She supposed if she were a different sort of person, a braver sort of person, she could defy James, refuse to marry him and bring up her child—their child—on her own; there had certainly been times since her visit to the doctor had confirmed what she had already secretly known in her heart—that she was carrying James's child—when she had toyed unrealistically with the idea of simply running away... disappearing... avoiding all the misery and anguish that she knew lay ahead of her.

But how could she? How could she hurt her parents by doing something like that? And besides, no matter where she ran to she could never escape from herself or from the knowledge of what she had done.

However, she could not face James yet, even though she was acutely conscious of the thoughtful looks her mother had been giving her and suspected that it wouldn't be long before she questioned her increasingly hard-to-conceal bouts of sickness and put two and two together.

There were alternatives, of course, she acknowledged tiredly as she prepared for her lunch date, but they were simply not options she could ever choose to take. Little though she had wanted or planned to have a baby—*any* baby, never mind James's—now that she knew that she actually *had* conceived... Poppy placed her hand protectively over her stomach. No, she couldn't do that, couldn't take away the life that she and James had created.

She knew why James had left that message on her private line, of course; she knew perfectly well what it was he wanted to ask her... The unexpected business commitment which had taken him abroad had meant that he had had to leave before he could question her about the outcome of her visit to the doctor and she knew she would have little alternative but to tell him.

The last thing she felt like doing today was going to lunch. What would the other two think if they knew that soon she would be breaking the vow that they had all made to remain unmarried? Would *they*, like her parents and her family, assume that she was actually in love with James? That all the years she had spent loving Chris had simply been a youthful infatuation which had really meant nothing?

It had shocked Poppy to discover that her parents, and especially her mother, seemed to think that James was so right for her—that they were so right for one another. Even Chris had told her how pleased he was for both of them. It seemed to Poppy that the only people who weren't pleased or happy about the fact that she and James had supposedly fallen deeply in love with one another were she and James themselves.

Oddly enough, instead of feeling hurt by Chris's comment, by his inability to see the truth, what Poppy had experienced had been a totally unexpected and disconcerting sense of irritation and exasperation...

The restaurant was quite quiet, the conservatory where they were lunching pleasantly cool, but Poppy still felt queasy and uncomfortably warm as she sat down.

She could see the faintly concerned looks that Claire, Sally's stepmother, was giving her as she toyed with her food and made monosyllabic responses to her conversation, but the smell of food was making her head swim and her stomach churn—or was it the fact that just being there was bringing home to her the enormity of what she had done and the way her life was bound to change?

Panic filled her as she realised how unprepared for change she really was. Unable to face another mouthful of food, she pushed away her plate and stood up.

Once she reached the sanctuary of the ladies' cloakroom she discovered that her nausea had subsided, and by the time Claire came in search of her she felt sufficiently in control of herself to apologise for her sudden exit, even if her voice did shake a little as she said the words.

What would they think once they discovered the truth, these two women with whom she had sworn a vow to remain unmarried and so disprove the myth of the potency of catching the bride's bouquet?

And, no matter how quickly she and James got married, once the baby arrived people were *bound* to guess the truth. Her face burned hotly. There was no onus on couples these days to marry before having children, and had she and James genuinely been in love she knew that her prime emotion on learning that she had conceived his child would have been one of intense joy and delight.

But they were *not* in love and she had conceived his child whilst believing ... whilst wanting another man, and that was the source of her shame and anguish, of her dread at the prospect of marriage to him.

She was relieved when the lunch was finally over. Having said goodbye to Star outside the restaurant, she and Claire were left alone together. As Claire turned to her, clearly about to say something, Poppy saw James's familiar Jaguar driving towards them, James himself at the wheel, and she froze, torn between her need to turn and flee and her knowledge that physically she felt incapable of moving so much as a muscle. The Jaguar stopped abruptly in front of them and James got out and strode towards them.

Poppy winced, and she felt James's fingers curl round her arm, locking on it in a grip that she couldn't break. 'James, what are you doing here? How did you know where to find me?'

'I looked in your diary,' he told her witheringly. 'Get in the car.'

'James ... I ...'

I don't want to go with you, she had been about to say, but he shook his head, telling her grimly, 'Not now, Poppy; I'm not in the mood for it. Where the hell have you been?' he demanded as he propelled her towards the Jaguar. 'Why the hell haven't you been in touch with me?'

As she turned towards him he warned her, 'No games, Poppy; you know what I mean, you know what it is I want to know...'

Just for a heartbeat Poppy contemplated lying to him, telling him that she wasn't pregnant after all, but the impulse soon died, shrivelled by the hot, dry blast of his anger.

'I was right, wasn't I?' James continued mercilessly, after he had bundled her into the car, slid into the driver's seat and set the car in motion. 'You *have* conceived my child.'

'Yes,' Poppy admitted tonelessly. Why, when she knew how little emotion there was between them, how lacking in tender, loving feelings their relationship was, did she have this urge to cry, to turn to James and beg him to stop the car and put his arms round her, hold her, make her feel safe...make her feel protected...make her feel loved?

She tensed her body, expecting his anger to accelerate at her confirmation of her pregnancy with the same velocity with which the car had increased speed, but instead he remained oddly quiet—so quiet in fact that Poppy felt impelled to turn her head and look at him—the first time she had looked at him since he had stopped the car and come striding so angrily towards her.

James wasn't paying any attention to her; his gaze, his concentration appeared to be fixed on the empty road ahead of them.

'I...I won't...I can't not have my baby,' she told him doggedly, realising only as she gave voice to the shaky words just how strongly she already felt about her child, how protective of it, how determined always to keep it from hurt and from harm.

Now James did look at her, and the look in his eyes made her wince slightly as he told her starkly, 'If I thought for one moment that you might...This baby is *mine* as well as yours, Poppy, and if I thought that you'd do anything—and I do mean *anything* to harm it...'

Poppy's body shook as she listened to him. That he would insist on them both 'doing the right thing' she had never doubted—he was that sort of man— but the emotion she had heard in his voice as he'd told her that the baby—her baby—was his child as well had left her lost for words, grappling with the shock of suddenly discovering a side to him that she had never imagined existed.

She knew, of course, how protective he could be towards his close family, but it had never occurred to her that those feelings might extend to a child he had never even intended should be conceived.

'We'll need to talk to your parents,' she heard him warning her, 'and then my mother...'

'Do we...are we...? They'll have to know the truth,' she told him, unaware of how haunted and unhappy she looked as she whispered rather than stated the words.

'Yes,' he agreed quietly. 'Or at least part of it. I warn you, Poppy, that not just for your own sake but for the baby's sake as well there is *one* truth that it is advisable that no one should ever know.'

Poppy's heart started to thump heavily as he turned his head to look at her.

'What... what do you mean?' she asked him, her mouth dry with foreboding.

'They must *never*—no one must *ever* have any reason to think that our child... our relationship... is the result of anything other than love.'

'Love?' Poppy swallowed hard as she stared at him aghast. 'But no one will really believe that. They all know the way I feel about Chris...'

'They all know that you had an adolescent crush on my brother,' James corrected her coldly.

'I can't pretend that I've fallen in love with you,' Poppy told him. 'No one would ever believe me.'

'No? Then you'll just have to find a way of *making* them believe you,' James informed her. 'Unless, of course, you actually want people to guess the truth.'

'No,' Poppy denied sharply, her face burning with hot colour.

'No,' James said sardonically. 'You're caught between two equally unpalatable choices, I'm afraid, Poppy. You either pretend you love me or you take the risk of people questioning why, if you don't, you and I conceived a child. It's a question of the lesser of two evils.'

'Chris will never believe that I've fallen in love with you,' Poppy protested feverishly.

'He is far too busy with his own life and his new wife to have any time to spare questioning what's going on in yours. Face it, Poppy, what you choose to do or not to do with your life isn't of much interest to Chris, other than as a cousin, and if anything—'

'He'll be only too relieved not to have the embarrassment of me loving him any more,' Poppy broke in shakily. 'Yes, so you've already told me.'

'Are both your parents at home this evening?'

'Yes—yes, I think so,' Poppy confirmed as she tried to grapple with the confusion of her thoughts. Part of her ached and longed to turn the clock back and to have things as they were, but if that were possible that would mean... Her hand moved automatically towards her stomach. The discovery of how emotionally attached she had become to the thought of her child in such a short space of time shocked her.

'Good. We'll need to talk to them as quickly as possible. I think so far as the general public is concerned the fact that the family has barely got over one big wedding should serve as a reasonable excuse for the haste of ours...'

'But people are bound to guess, especially once the baby—'

'So let them guess,' James shrugged as he shot back his cuff to glance at his watch. 'I'll come round about eight,' he told her as he brought the car to a halt outside her parents' house.

Poppy reached numbly for the doorhandle. She felt tired and drained, alone, and even afraid. This wasn't how she had imagined things would be... how her life, her marriage would be. And never, ever in her darkest nightmares had she envisaged a scenario so starkly devoid of love and emotion.

James had got out and was now standing on the pavement beside her. As the panic flared inside her she turned towards him.

'We can't marry one another, James,' she protested. 'We don't love each other. We have nothing in common, nothing to keep us together, nothing to make our marriage real.'

All her fears and her pent-up sense of loss and anguish were contained in her voice and her expression as she turned pleadingly towards him, but James ignored them, taking hold of her right there in her parents' drive, his hands firm and compelling as he gripped her upper arms and told her savagely, 'No! We've got this much, Poppy.'

And then he was kissing her, his mouth hard and warm on hers, burning the numb immobility of her lips into fierce, painful life as they softened and then clung to his, his touch conjuring up inside her a sharp, whirlwind sensation and taut, aching need.

Their surroundings, their situation, everything else faded into insignificance as Poppy clung helplessly to him whilst her body responded to his touch, his kiss.

When he finally released her, it took her several seconds to realise where they were and why. Tears glittered brightly in her eyes as she started to turn away from him, her face hot with shame. *Why* was it that she responded so immediately and so physically to him? *Why ...?*

'Poppy,' she heard him saying when she made to walk away. The sound of his voice halted her and she turned automatically to face him. 'We've also got this,' he reminded her, one hand on her arm, the other, fingers spread, placed against her stomach.

She could feel the warmth of his touch through her clothes—male and somehow oddly possessive—and even though she knew it was impossible Poppy could have sworn that the new life within her responded somehow to his touch, knew it almost.

Head bowed, she stood there unresisting as the tears again filled her eyes like liquid crystals. She could feel James moving towards her, closing the gap between them. She could feel the warmth of his breath as he bent his head towards her, and the fear that he might kiss her again, might bring back the wretched, treacherous surge of desire that he seemed to summon up within her so effortlessly lent her the impetus to push away from him and half run towards the sanctuary of the house.

'I'm afraid that I'm really the one to blame.' James's hand reached out and took hold of Poppy's. His grip felt oddly comforting, warming the icy chill of her own nervously tense fingers.

James had just finished telling her parents that they intended to marry as soon as they could—and why. The silence which had followed his announcement had caused Poppy to hang her head in shame as she'd waited for the blow to fall and for her parents to demand to know how she came to be carrying James's child when they both knew how much she loved Chris, but to her astonishment neither of them made any such comment. Instead, they hugged her lovingly whilst her father cleared his throat.

'Oh, darling, I always knew that eventually you and James would sort out your differences, although I must admit, I didn't expect it to happen quite so—'

'It's my fault,' James repeated, gently tugging Poppy towards him so that she had no alternative but to allow him to draw her into the protection of his body.

And he told her parents with an apparent sincerity that had Poppy holding her breath and staring up at him in wide-eyed disbelief, 'Having waited for so long, having loved and wanted her for so long, once Poppy... Well, let's just say that I let my feelings get the better of me without fully thinking through the potential consequences. And, wrongly or not, I can't pretend that the end result isn't one that fills me with great joy, even though for the sake of conformity I should have taken steps...

'My main concern in all of this is that Poppy isn't upset and that you'll forgive me for depriving you of the opportunity to spend the next twelve months organising our wedding,' he told Poppy's mother wryly.

'Well, I must admit that you have rather surprised us,' Poppy's mother confessed, 'although... Don't look like that, darling,' she reassured Poppy. 'I do remember how it feels to be so very much in love, you know,' she said gently. 'Your father and I...'

Poppy's father coughed again, making her mother laugh.

'It will have to be a quiet family wedding, of course; have you made any plans? Poppy will need a dress, of course, and then there'll be the wedding breakfast...'

'No,' Poppy protested. 'I...' She flushed as both her parents looked at her. 'I won't need a dress,' she told them huskily. 'Not for a register office wedding. I—'

'It won't *be* a register office wedding,' James interrupted her curtly. 'We'll be getting married in church,' he told her mother, to Poppy's shock.

And then, before Poppy could say anything, he cupped her face in one hand and there, in full view of her parents, turned it up towards his own, kissing her lightly on the tip of her nose and then far more lingeringly on her mouth before saying softly, 'I don't want anyone thinking that either of us regrets what's happened or that our child isn't welcome and a wanted addition to our lives. And I certainly don't want them thinking that our marriage is anything other than a celebration of the love we feel for one another and for him or her.'

It wasn't until he kissed the moisture from the corners of her eyes that Poppy realised she was crying. As James released her she saw that her mother's eyes looked suspiciously damp as well.

'I can't wear a white dress,' she told her mother shakily. 'It will have to be—'

'Ivory or cream,' her mother agreed, apparently totally misunderstanding her. 'White has never been a good colour for you. I remember when I was buying your christening robe...

'If it's just going to be a family affair, James, I think we should have the wedding breakfast here. We'll have it catered, of course. Have you told your own mother yet?'

'No, Poppy and I are going to see her later.'

This was news to Poppy but she had no energy left to argue. She was still shaken by James's ability to lie so convincingly. If she hadn't known better, even *she* would have been taken in by the little performance he had just put on for her parents.

And she couldn't help thinking how much, if she had genuinely loved James, those words, that confirmation of his commitment to her and to their child would have meant to her. It struck Poppy all at once how little she actually thought about Chris these days, but then she had hardly had the luxury of having the *time* to think about him, had she? Before, when there had been no James in her life, no plans to make for the future, no other matters to concern her, she had had the leisure to indulge in as many daydreams about Chris and how it would be if he loved her as she wished.

And besides, it seemed wrong somehow, unfair to her unborn child to indulge in the immaturity of day-dreaming about a man she could never have—a man who was not that child's father.

It shocked her a little bit that her parents should so easily accept the supposed transfer of her love from Chris to James.

She *had* loved Chris.

Had loved him?

For some reason Poppy felt as though she was suddenly standing on the edge of a very deep and dangerous chasm which had totally unexpectedly opened virtually beneath her unsuspecting feet.

'Ready?' she heard James asking her.

She swallowed nervously. Ready for what? For the future—their future? How *could* she be when it wasn't a future she would have chosen for herself?

Six weeks after, they were married in church with her wearing an ivory lace and silk wedding dress which had originally been made for James's Italian great-grandmother. The dress had been a gift from James's aunt, who had travelled from her home in Rome especially to bring it and, Poppy suspected, to congratulate her on her good taste and good fortune in marrying her favourite relative.

It had only had to be let out a little bit at the waist. Her pregnancy might not be showing physically in her body as yet, Poppy acknowledged as she stood mutely

at James's side after the ceremony, his wife now and
no longer just his cousin, but she suspected that the
time she had had off work with the debilitating bouts
of sickness which had accompanied the early weeks
of pregnancy had alerted most people to the reality
of the situation.

However, no one had actually said anything, apart
from Sally, who had commented rather enviously
earlier in the day as she'd helped Poppy to dress for
her wedding, 'Chris and I said that we would wait a
few years before we started a family. I thought that
was what I wanted but now... I suppose there's
something about conceiving a child by the man you
love that adds a special depth to your relationship...a special closeness. You only have to look
at how happy Claire and Brad are,' she said wistfully,
'now that they're married and expecting a baby...'

Poppy hadn't known what to say. How *could* she
tell Sally of all people the truth? And now it was too
late to tell anyone anything. Now she and James were
married, husband and wife, a couple, a pair...parents-
in-waiting.

Poppy shivered, closing her eyes as she remembered the moment when James had lifted the heavy
antique veil from her face to look at her in absolute
silence, before raising his hands to cup her face.

Her whole body had trembled so much that it had
even felt as though his hands were trembling as he'd
bent his head and then slowly kissed her, not with
sensual passion, not with any emotion she could put
a name to or recognise, but with something else—
something in the way he'd looked at her, something
in the solemnity of the vows they had just taken that

had brought a lump to her throat and made her lips quiver beneath his.

Had anyone other than she noticed the way his fingers had gently brushed her stomach as he'd released her face, his touch as much a wordless, secret promise to their child as his vows had been a public one to her?

Poppy doubted it; *that* gesture had not been for public view; that gesture, that vow had been something private between James and his son...or daughter— something which she'd felt at that moment had actually excluded her. It had also made her acutely conscious of the reason why they were marrying and of the fiction of James's public display of love for her.

Chris came up to them now, to envelop his brother in a bear-hug of emotion and to give Poppy a wide, beaming grin. His hair needed cutting and the way it flopped into his eyes made him look both boyish and slightly bashful.

As she listened to Sally scolding him lovingly for unfastening the top button of his shirt and removing his tie, Poppy wondered what would have happened if it *had* been Chris's child she was carrying and not James's; how *would* Chris have reacted in such circumstances? She tried to envisage him calmly taking control as James had done, seeing her parents, explaining what had happened to them, taking the blame and the responsibility, and she was forced to acknowledge that if Chris had been the father it would have been more likely that *she* would have been the one to take charge, to do the explaining...to take the blame.

'Stop it,' she heard James telling her warningly. Then he said, 'It's me you're married to, Poppy, not Chris. My child you're carrying—mine!'

'Don't you think I *know* that?' she returned bitterly. Her dress suddenly felt uncomfortably tight round her waist, her head ached and she felt hot and tired.

'I hate all this hypocrisy,' she told James angrily. 'All this pretence.'

'Really? You didn't seem to mind the pretence the night you convinced yourself you were in bed with Chris and not with me,' James reminded her bluntly.

Shocked by the unexpectedness of his attack, coming so soon after his convincing act of love in church, Poppy could only stare at him in silence until she was rescued by the welcome sound of her mother's voice exclaiming, 'Darling, are you all right? You look rather pale. Come and sit down. Everyone's here now and the caterers are ready to serve lunch.'

CHAPTER EIGHT

'IT WON'T be long now.'

Poppy had balked at the idea of a honeymoon but James had insisted, pointing out that it would look odd if they didn't go away, and in the end she had had to give in, although she had wished she hadn't when he had told her where they were going.

'Italy!' she had protested. 'No, I can't, not Italy; it will remind me of your Japanese friend—the one you spent the night with at the hotel,' she had begun, childishly driven into the panicky reaction by her own misery.

But James had stopped her, telling her firmly, 'The only person I spent the night with at the hotel was you.'

'One night you didn't come back to the room,' Poppy had accused him challengingly.

'Yes, but not because I was with someone else. If you must know, I stayed up all night working.'

Poppy hadn't quite been able to bring herself to look at him. 'I still don't want to go back to Italy.'

'We don't have much choice,' James had told her coolly. 'My mother is insisting on giving us the villa as a wedding gift and it would look churlish to refuse.'

Poppy had known he was right. James's mother had not used the villa since James's father's death, preferring, she said, to keep her happy memories of the holidays they had spent there intact.

Now she had told James and Poppy it was time that other members of the family enjoyed it, and since James had always been far more in touch with his Italian heritage than Chris she had decided that James and Poppy should have it.

Poppy had been there once with her parents, as a child, and she remembered how awed she had been by the Tuscan countryside, by the richness of its colours and the warm vibrancy of its people and its life.

One unexpected side effect of her pregnancy had been that her body temperature seemed to have risen by several degrees, and the air-conditioning in the car that James had hired for them was a welcome antidote to the heat of the Italian summer, beneath which the Tuscan countryside drowsed.

Whenever Poppy thought of the area she always thought of it in terms of its colours—amber, saffron, warm browns and rich terracotta—the colours of the earth, colours which, for her, echoed its richness and warmth, its bounty, their depth leavened and lightened by the cerulean sky.

The villa—their villa now—was small and relatively isolated and had originally been a wedding gift from James's father to his mother.

'James was conceived there,' she had told Poppy several days ago, 'and I've often wondered if that is why he is so much more in tune with his Italian heritage than Chris.

'You do love him, don't you, Poppy?' she had asked quietly. 'Because I know how much he loves you, how much he has always loved you.' And Poppy had bowed her head.

She had no idea why, when James could so obviously and easily lie to his mother, she seemed unable to do the same, but perhaps her aunt had taken the tears in her eyes as a sign of her love for James rather than the reverse, Poppy decided, because she had not pressed the matter, simply touching Poppy's bent head gently.

The small town several miles away from the villa was just as Poppy remembered it. A couple of dark-eyed children watched them from an open doorway as they drove past and Poppy's heart turned over, seized by the quick, melting surge of emotions she had become familiar with in these last weeks.

'What is it? What's wrong?' James asked her, but she did not feel able to tell him, to explain.

Did all women feel like this when they knew they were carrying a child? she wondered. Did they all experience this—this emotional awareness of the vulnerability of all young things, this need to protect and cherish? The strength of her love for a child she had never intended to conceive, the bond she felt with it already, constantly amazed her. She might not love *James* or he her, but she would—she did even now—love their child.

And so did James, she acknowledged, moving her head to look at him as he turned off the main road and onto the narrow dirt track that led to the villa.

Time and the hot Tuscan sun had turned the original deep terracotta of the building into a soft, faded colour somewhere between pink and brown. The shutters, closed now against the afternoon sun, were painted white. The local farmer whom James's mother paid to maintain the property for her had obviously repainted them recently, Poppy decided as she noted their dazzling brilliance.

James stopped the car and got out. Uncertainly Poppy went to join him.

'Paolo should have been down with some supplies for us,' he told her, referring to the farmer. 'If not, I'll leave you to get settled in and drive back to the village to get some. Is there anything in particular that you would like?'

'Only water,' Poppy told him, grimacing a little. Her mouth, like her body, felt dry and dusty from the journey. The heat, coupled with her own inner tension, had also made her feel slightly light-headed. As she blinked dizzily in the sun, she saw that James was frowning.

'You'd better get inside out of the heat,' he told her.

'I'm pregnant, James, that's all,' she responded irritably. 'There's no need to fuss. Not that you *are* fussing—fussing on *my* account,' she added bitterly. 'You don't give a damn what happens to me.'

'Would you want me to?'

Poppy stiffened as she heard the challenge in his voice.

'We both know what's really bugging you, Poppy,' James added grimly, 'and it isn't my so-called "fussing", is it? For God's sake!' he exclaimed, 'I know I'm not Chris but just when the hell are you going to grow up and realise—?' He stopped, rubbing the back of his neck with his hand and frowning as he narrowed his eyes against the sun.

'Let's get inside,' he told her, turning towards the front door to the villa.

Silently Poppy followed him, deliberately keeping her distance as he unlocked the weathered wooden door. Inside the villa it felt blissfully cool. Whilst James opened the shutters Poppy made her way to the kitchen. Paolo had obviously been, because there was a box of groceries on the kitchen table. As she looked through it Poppy sniffed appreciatively at the locally cured ham and the freshly picked tomatoes, suddenly feeling unexpectedly hungry.

'Aha, you like that, do you?' she teased the baby, speaking her thoughts out loud as her mouth watered at the sight and smell of the fresh, locally baked bread.

'You're going to be like your *papà*, are you, and favour your Italian heritage?' she laughed as her tiredness melted away, her body relaxing now that it was released from the tension of James's constant presence. It was something new that she had only started very recently, this verbal communication with her child.

'Well, don't expect me to be a doting Italian *mamma* and spoil you,' she warned with very obvious untruth. Then spinning round, her face flushing, she realised that James was standing in the doorway. How long had he been there? Long enough to overhear her silliness, she guessed, and quickly defended herself.

'All the books say that it's important to communicate with the baby even before it's born, to let it know that you're there, that you care, that you love it.'

'And do you love it... him or her?'

'He or she is my child... How could I not do?' Poppy demanded huskily.

'Your child is also mine,' James reminded her. '*Mine*, Poppy,' he reiterated. 'And, let me warn you now, if you ever, *ever* attempt to pretend that my child has my brother for its father, in the same way you pretended that he was your lover—'

'Paolo doesn't seem to have brought us any milk,' Poppy told him, quickly turning away, not wanting him to see the flush burning her face.

'Poppy,' James warned.

'No... no, I shall never try to pretend Chris is my... our baby's father,' she said. 'Not to myself or to anyone else.

'James, how are we going to endure this?' she demanded starkly, turning back to face him, her eyes betraying her misery. 'We don't love each other.' Her voice quickened with panic. 'We don't even like one another.'

'We'll endure it because we have to, because of him or her,' James told her grimly, his glance resting tellingly on her stomach before he picked up the car keys which he had dropped on the table. 'I'll take the cases upstairs and then I'll go down to the village for some water. I'll put your luggage in the main bedroom—I'll sleep in the other one...'

The villa only had two bedrooms, both of them very spacious, and one bathroom, which was off the larger of the two rooms so that whoever was using the smaller had to walk through the main bedroom to get to it. James's mother had always said that one day she would add a second bathroom, but she had never got round to it.

Without waiting for her to answer, James walked towards the door.

The rear of the villa was shaded by a vine-covered patio. The summer that Poppy had stayed here with her parents they had eaten most of their meals on it.

How on earth was she going to endure two weeks cooped up alone here with James? And if she couldn't bear the thought of spending *two weeks* alone with him, then how was she going to get through all the years that lay ahead of them? Tiredly she went upstairs.

Paolo's wife had made up both beds on James's instructions. How had he explained the fact that a honeymooning couple required two double beds? Poppy wondered dully as she stripped off her clothes and showered off the dirt of their drive before pulling on clean underwear and crawling beneath the lavender-scented linen sheets.

Poppy smiled contentedly to herself as she slipped on her soft lawn cotton dress and glanced out of the bedroom window. The sky was a perfect, clear blue, promising another sunny day.

It was just as she let the loose folds of her dress fall round her hips and started to straighten up that she felt it—no more than the briefest flutter of sensation—a movement as delicate as the touch of a flower petal falling against her skin. She recognised it straight away, instinctively, calling out automatically, without thinking, 'James . . . quick . . .'

'What is it? What's wrong?' he demanded as he responded to her summons, pushing open her bedroom door and standing watching her.

She had dreaded this time—being isolated from everyone else, being alone with James, knowing that it was bound to reveal all the flaws in their relationship, all the reasons why they should not have married, and yet astonishingly the days had actually passed very quickly.

Her body, perhaps exhausted by the trauma of the weeks leading up to the wedding, had wanted only to relax and absorb the heat of the sun. Her instincts had caused her to focus not on the antipathy which existed between her and James but on her need to protect the life growing within her, and, yes, there had been times, moments when she had been heart-wrenchingly conscious of all that she had forfeited, all that she would never have—all that both of them had forfeited, she acknowledged, in committing themselves to a marriage without love—and then she had ached with pain and an intense but nebulous sense of loss and despair.

And yet, oddly, it had not been Chris whom she'd thought of at such times—his image, the memories of him cherished all through the years of her adolescence seemed to have lost their old power to give her succour.

'What is it?' James repeated, frowning.

As she looked back at him, noticing how very masculine he looked in a pair of soft, natural-coloured linen shorts and white T-shirt, his legs bare and very brown, his forearms surprisingly strongly muscled for a man who spent so much of his time seated at a desk, Poppy felt a sharp pang of unexpected emotion, an unexpected and devastating awareness of how intensely male James actually was.

It was, she felt, as though suddenly she was seeing him in a different way, as though she had walked into a room in which all the familiar objects had been moved around so that she saw them with fresh eyes—saw them and found that she had allowed habit to conceal the true depth of their appeal from her.

Her heart suddenly seemed to beat a little bit faster and she knew that she had flushed slightly.

'Don't you feel very well?' James was asking her. For the first few days of their stay he had insisted that she remain in bed in the morning until he had brought her a cup of tea and some plain biscuits.

Initially she had been irritated by such coddling, telling him curtly that she knew it was for the baby's sake and not hers, but these last couple of mornings she had actually found that she was quite enjoying being spoiled—a feeling which had sneaked up on her, catching her unawares.

'No. No, I feel fine...'

Now that he was here, frowning at her, obviously irritated at being interrupted, she was beginning to regret the impulse which had led to her calling him, and besides...

'It was nothing,' she told him, starting to turn away from him. 'I was just wondering if you still intended to go into town later on.'

'Yes, we need petrol and food and—'

He broke off as Poppy suddenly gave a small, startled gasp, hurrying to her side, his frown deepening as he touched her on one slim brown arm and said, 'Poppy, if you're not feeling well...'

'No, it isn't that,' she denied, her flush deepening to a happy glow of pleasure as she told him breathlessly, 'It's the baby; it's moving... Feel,' she added impetuously, taking hold of his hand and placing it on her body.

When she felt his resistance she immediately let go of him, snatching her fingers away from his as though the contact had burned her, quick, emotional tears she couldn't conceal filling her eyes as she tried to move back from him. Only James wouldn't let her, and, despite his initial withdrawal, his hand was now lying against her body, firm and warm and somehow oddly comforting and reassuring.

The baby must have thought so too, she decided hazily, because it suddenly shifted much more vigorously than it had before, causing Poppy to laugh out loud in maternal pride as she saw the look of mingled disbelief and awe in James's eyes.

An unfamiliar tinge of colour was darkening his face, making him look somehow different and vulnerable. He had lowered his head slightly, his gaze fixed on where his hand lay against her, and Poppy had an odd and devastating urge to reach out and hold him.

As she tried to absorb the full implications of what she was experiencing it seemed to Poppy that somehow or other the foundations of her whole world had shifted dangerously beneath her, leaving her very afraid and alone.

'Feels like she's going to inherit your talent for making her presence felt,' was James's only comment as he removed his hand and stepped back from her, but although his voice was steady Poppy could see how moved he was by what he had experienced.

'She?' she queried, her own voice husky. 'You want it to be a girl, then?'

'Yes,' James confirmed, his voice becoming familiarly harsh. He added, 'At least that way...' He shook his head, his mouth clamping shut on what he had been about to say.

It surprised Poppy that he should want a daughter; she had imagined that a man like James would only value sons. Despite the fact that they were cousins, she knew surprisingly little about him as a man, she recognised, but she was learning.

Oh, yes, she was learning, she acknowledged later in the day, lying in a chair in the garden, waiting for James to return from his trip into town. And not just about James.

The odd feelings that she had experienced this morning—that shaft of pure, liquid desire that had shot through her when she'd seen him standing in the bedroom doorway, that flood of heart-rocking emotion that had swamped her as she'd watched him reaching out to make contact with their child...

Frantically she tried to control and dismiss them by comparing them with the love she had always felt for Chris, but somehow it was impossible for her to summon up anything more than a faint echo of the emotion which had dominated her entire life for so many years.

Even picturing Chris was an effort, and when she did the face that looked back at her through her imagination was simply that of her cousin and not her adored, longed-for lover. Her body and her heart were empty of the intensity of yearning that she had expected to feel.

Was it her pregnancy that was responsible for her lack of physical and emotional desire for Chris? She had desired James only a few hours earlier, she admitted, and she desired him now.

She moved her body uncomfortably on the sun-lounger but the torrent of heat engulfing her had nothing to do with the strength of the sun. She sat up, her face burning with the shock of her discovery. She couldn't want James. It was impossible.

But she wasn't an innocent girl any more; she was a woman—a woman who knew perfectly well how her body reacted when it was aroused, when it wanted and desired. There was no mistaking such signals, no confusing them with something else.

But James, of all men. Was it something to do with the fact that they had already been lovers?

Instinctively Poppy looked towards the front of the villa, searching for some sign of his return, her heart racing. She wanted James to come back, Poppy acknowledged; she felt vulnerable without him, afraid of her own feelings and what they might mean, alienated from her past and apprehensive about her future.

It might be the baby who was responsible for her see-sawing emotions, she tried to reassure herself; it had to be... And for her physical desire...?

'We'd better make a move if you want to eat out tonight,' James warned Poppy.

She was still sitting outside, watching the sun set, or so she told herself. In truth, since James had returned from town, she had actually been surreptitiously watching him, frantically trying to mask her avid need to keep him within sight as she desperately tried to understand what was happening to her.

Why, why should the most mundane of normal human attributes, such as the way he walked, the sheen of his skin, the fluid ease of his movements, even the warm brown curve of his throat, suddenly evoke such intense feelings and needs within her? Why, when she had known him all her life, should she suddenly have become so suffocatingly aware of him that he had only to come within five yards of her for her heart to beat frantically fast?

And why, when she had never, ever even thought such a thing before, should the mere idea of him touching her bring the tiny hairs up all over her body whilst her skin itself tingled in a silent agony of aching demand?

She had no answer to such questions, Poppy acknowledged soberly, there was no answer...

'I'll go and get changed,' she said now in response to James's comment and went indoors.

The sun had turned her skin a soft, warm peach-gold; her tan was much lighter and more delicate than James's. It must surely be her pregnancy that had given her flesh such a rounded feel and such a healthy glow, she thought as she caught sight of herself in the bedroom mirror.

Although the baby had barely started to show as much more than a slight swell, she was already beginning to feel more comfortable in softer clothes, and was glad now that she had let Sally persuade her into a pre-wedding shopping spree.

The fluid ice-cream-coloured dresses that Sally had chosen were not her normal style but oddly they seemed to suit her, although she had never thought of herself as being feminine enough to wear thin muslins that drifted over her body, sleeveless and scoop-necked so that they showed her tanned arms and clung subtly to the slightly fuller curves of her breasts.

'These will be wonderfully cool,' Sally had enthused. 'All you'll need to wear under them is a pair of briefs. Try this one,' she had insisted, rummaging along the rail and producing a fine, soft mint-green cotton dress with a drop waist and inverted pleats, which buttoned down the front.

'Oh, yes!' Sally had exclaimed when Poppy had reluctantly put it on. 'James will enjoy that . . . all those buttons. Men love buttons . . .'

Poppy remembered how her hands had trembled as she'd wrenched it off. She had decided not to buy it but somehow or other Sally had managed to get it included in her purchases, a fact which she had not discovered until it was too late and she had got it home.

Now, having showered, her hands trembled again as she put it on, but this time for a different reason.

'James will enjoy that . . .' Sally had said, and the sheer intensity of the surge of sensation that hit her as she closed her eyes and pictured him reaching for those small buttons, unfastening them to reveal the curves of her naked body, made Poppy shudder from head to foot and cry out against its torment.

'Poppy . . . ?'

As she opened her eyes, her face flushing, she realised that James must have heard her.

'What is it? Is it the baby? Is something wrong?'

He walked towards her, his own torso bare, the cream linen trousers that he had pulled on so softly shaped that they revealed the taut hardness of his thighs as he moved.

Poppy watched him, mesmerised, her lips slightly parted as she absorbed every movement.

'James.'

He had come close enough for her to touch him now and dizzily she did so, lifting her hand to his arm and her glance to meet his, her eyes already darkening with need and desire.

'I want you,' she told him unsteadily. 'I want you, James. I . . .'

'Poppy...' he began, but she didn't want to hear what she knew he was going to say, her body trembling as her fingers tightened on his arm.

'No, no...I don't want you to say anything. I just want... James, I'm so afraid,' she told him shakily. 'I don't understand what's happening to me...why I should...'

She could feel him starting to pull away from her, his body tense.

She began to tremble, afraid both of being close to him, because of her desire for him, and of being apart from him, because he was the only stable, familiar thing in a world which had suddenly become alien and out of control.

As he leaned towards her, her lips inadvertently touched his skin, igniting her desire into a fireball of wrenching need. She moaned his name and started to press desperate, hungry kisses against his chest and throat, her control swamped by the scent and taste of him, by the feel of his skin beneath her mouth, the way he swallowed as her lips feverishly caressed his throat, the way his hands tightened on her shoulders as he reached out for her—not to push her away but to draw her nearer.

The thud of his heartbeat beneath her palm suddenly accelerated and his hand curved round the back of her neck, moving her slowly, guiding the clinging moistness of her mouth over his skin whilst his fingers tightened in her hair and he said something roughly under his breath.

And then suddenly he was the one kissing her, cupping her face and holding her immobile whilst his mouth covered hers. What was it about a certain man's kiss that was so sensually arousing, so impossible to resist? Poppy wondered dizzily as her mouth clung passionately to his, opened hotly beneath his, inviting the swift, fierce invasion of his tongue, her whole body shuddering in response to the effect that he was having on her.

Aching, she pressed herself closer to him, aware of his own arousal through the barriers of their clothes, wanting to be even closer to him, wanting...

'James, my dress...' As she whispered the words against his mouth, she opened her eyes and looked up into the brilliance of his. It felt as if she was looking right into the sun, she acknowledged dizzily, only even more dangerous.

She could feel the heat of her reaction to him flooding her body, filling it, making her ache for a different kind of fullness, a different fulfilment that could only come from him, from his touch, from his body. She could see him frowning as he started to look down her body at her dress, as though not understanding what she wanted.

'Take it off,' she whispered. 'I want to feel you next to me, James... All of you,' she insisted huskily.

Without knowing she had done so, she had already lifted his hand to the front of her dress, to its buttons, and now she watched, her body still, taut with aching anticipation, as he slowly reached out and started to unfasten them, his gaze never leaving hers as they slowly slid free.

When he reached the buttons that secured the dress across her breasts Poppy started to tremble. She was wearing nothing underneath.

'What is it you want from me, Poppy?' James asked her rawly, stopping what he was doing whilst he waited for her answer.

'You know what I want,' Poppy whispered back.

'Show me,' he demanded.

Boldly Poppy did so, taking his hand and placing it on her bare breast. The feel of his hand against her body, cupping the smooth warmth of her, his thumb-tip slowly caressing her already hard nipple, made her shiver with aching pleasure, her eyes closing as she leaned yearningly towards him, her spine arching.

'What is it you want, Poppy?' she heard him mutter hoarsely as his mouth caressed her throat and then started to move lower.

'Is it this...? This...?'

'Yes. Oh, yes... Yes. Yes, James...' Poppy responded, the words subsiding into a moan of relief as his lips finally covered a nipple, playing delicately with it at first, as though he was holding back, afraid of being too passionate with her and hurting her. But the increased sensitivity of the fullness of her breasts only made her ache more for the hot suckle of his mouth that her body could still remember.

She moved urgently against him, showing him without words what she wanted, clasping her hands behind his head as she held him against her body, unable to keep the spasms of pleasure from rippling betrayingly through her as she cried out to him that she couldn't bear any more, that she was afraid of the pleasure he was giving her, afraid of the intensity of what she was experiencing.

But James didn't appear to be listening to her. Instead his mouth was caressing her body, kissing every inch of the flesh he exposed as he continued unfastening her buttons, pausing only when he reached the small swell of her belly, his hand covering the place where the child rested. He lifted his face to look at her and then, without a word, picked her up and carried her over to the bed, pushing her dress off her shoulders so that it slid to the floor before he laid her gently down.

For a long time he simply looked at her, and to Poppy, who had never once in her whole life imagined any man looking at her like that, never mind James, it came as a shocking revelation to recognise that instead of wanting to cover herself from him, instead of feeling self-conscious about her nakedness, she felt a sense of pride and joy in knowing that he was looking at her, in knowing just why his glance kept on returning to her gently rounded belly, in knowing just by looking at him that the sight of her aroused him.

She had never guessed that it was possible for a woman to feel so sexually strong, so sexually powerful and yet, at the same time, so vulnerable, so much in need, achingly soft and ready inside.

'James...'

She released his name on a soft, yearning sigh, reaching out her arms to him and then stopping, her face flushing tellingly as she whispered to him, 'Take off your clothes. I...I want to see you.'

For a moment she thought he might refuse, but then, as she saw the expression in his eyes, she realised that something in what she had said had touched him, reached him on some deeply personal level, almost as though her words had pleased him emotionally as well as physically.

Unblinkingly she watched as he unfastened his belt and then removed his clothes, her eyes wide, her face hot as she absorbed every detail of him.

It shocked her to feel an unmistakable frisson of female pride and smugness in knowing that, powerful and male though his body was, it could still be contained within hers, aroused by hers . . . as it was now.

She wanted to reach out and touch him but he was already leaning over her, bending his head as he gently kissed the small dome of her stomach.

The sensation of his mouth circling her navel was so unexpectedly erotic that her eyes widened still further at the shock of it, her body starting to tremble as she felt him removing her briefs.

How was it that whereas such a very short space of time ago she could not possibly have envisaged him touching her this kind of intimacy between them now—just the accidental touch of his hands against her skin—was enough to arouse her to the point where she was shamefully aware of just how ready her body was for him?

So ready that there was no point in dissembling, in acting out some kind of coy mock reluctance, in doing anything other than reaching out helplessly towards him and closing her eyes with a shuddering sigh of ecstasy as he took hold of her and slowly fitted his body to hers, his actions, his movements controlled and gentle and yet, at the same time, so strongly powerful that her body was convulsing with light spasms of pleasure just at the feel of him within her.

James made love to her again later, this time with his mouth and not with his body, easily disproving her assertion that she was already satisfied.

And then, before he could stop her, she, with great daring, did the same for him, shocked by the intensity of her own pleasure when he cried out beneath the untutored caress of her hands and mouth, trying to stop her before being overpowered by her gentle insistence and his own flooding desire.

For the first time Poppy slept within the curve of his arm, her sleepy mind knowing that such intimacy felt good and yet warning her at the same time that such feelings made her very vulnerable. But Poppy was too relaxed, too sleepy to heed that warning.

CHAPTER NINE

'WHEN I look at you, I'm not so sure that Chris and I made the right decision in opting not to start our family for a few years,' Sally commented enviously to Poppy as they shopped together one Saturday afternoon, reiterating the sentiment she'd expressed on the day of Poppy and James's wedding.

She stopped to draw Poppy's attention to the window of a small, exclusive babywear boutique before continuing hesitantly, 'It's different for you and James, I know. For one thing, James is so much more...so much more ready to be a father than Chris. You can tell how pleased he is about the baby.'

'Yes,' Poppy agreed quietly.

And it was true. There was no doubt that James wanted and already loved his child, but he certainly didn't feel the same way about its mother. Ever since that time in Italy when she had begged him to make love to her, he had held her at a distance, becoming so remote from her that now, six weeks later, it was virtually impossible for Poppy to imagine that they had ever been lovers; but these were things she couldn't say to Sally, who believed that they were deeply in love, or to anyone else.

The reality of her marriage was a secret she had to keep from everyone, the reality of her feelings for James a secret she had to keep from him—a secret she had had to keep from him ever since they had last been together, last made love!

She could still remember how it had felt to wake up in the morning with James beside her, to experience that extraordinary, purifying rush of love and self-knowledge, to reach out to touch him with it shining in her eyes and then to have *him* wake up and turn away from her, rebuff her, reject her.

And she had thought back to the evening before and been filled with mortification at the way she had behaved, the things she had done, the things she had said, and, even more painful to endure, the way she had felt.

She suspected now that she must have known the truth then, even though she had refused to acknowledge it. Certainly now when she looked back there seemed to be no other reason for what she had done, but in mitigation she had to admit that it would have been hard for the girl she had been—the girl who had stubbornly and publicly insisted that she could only love one man and that that man was Chris—to confess that she had been wrong and that everyone else had been right, that she had confused infatuation with love and that when she had finally discovered the difference it had been too late to turn back the clock.

If only she could. The pain of her infatuation for Chris was nothing when compared with the agony of heart and soul that she was enduring now, knowing that she loved James and knowing equally well that he did not love her.

She knew quite well why James had suddenly decided that he needed to spend so much more time away, take so many overnight business trips, and it had nothing to do with the fact, as everyone else seemed to suppose, that he wanted to clear some time to be with her and their baby, to be with her for his or her birth and in the weeks afterwards.

She supposed that it was another indication that she had finally, if somewhat belatedly, joined the real, adult world that she had not even tried to question James about his actions, about his withdrawal and his silence; that she had simply bowed her head and accepted the fact that he did not love her.

She was too aware now to attempt to deceive herself into believing that he might somehow, implausibly, fall in love with her as she had done with Chris. He wouldn't. And knowing that she loved him, knowing just why her body ached so much with wanting him, had also made it impossible for her to try to reach out to him physically through sex. It would be like drinking contaminated water—initially thirst-quenching but also potentially harmful, destructive, carrying with it the power to destroy her.

Having sex with James might temporarily ease the physical ache within her body, but it wouldn't satisfy her emotional need for him, and could, in fact, only underline it. And so she had rigidly enforced a strict control over herself, keeping as much physical distance between her and James as she could, in public as well as in private. And only on the nights when he wasn't there did she allow herself the luxury of tears, of crying herself to sleep. But then there were plenty of those.

She wondered tiredly what excuses he would make for being away so much once the baby was born. No doubt he would think of something and she would smile and concentrate her love on their baby, knowing that for as long as their marriage lasted he or she would be her only outlet for it.

James was due to go away again this evening and she had deliberately delayed returning from her shopping trip with Sally so that he would have left before she got home.

Automatically she found herself driving more slowly as she approached the house, dreading seeing his car. Thankfully it wasn't there. Relieved, Poppy parked her own car and hurried into the house. Despite the fact that she hadn't wanted him to be there, the house felt achingly empty without him, like her heart...like her life.

She had just finished making herself a cup of tea when she heard the doorbell ring. Frowning, she went to answer it, and was surprised to see Chris standing outside.

'Come in,' she invited. 'James isn't here but...'

'It's you I've come to see,' he told her, looking slightly awkward.

Poppy frowned again. Since her marriage to James she and Chris had not really been alone together. She winced, remembering how, on her return from honeymoon, she had not even noticed that Chris was away from the office until James had commented on the fact.

'It's...it's about Sally,' Chris told her after he had followed her into the kitchen and she had poured him a cup of tea.

'Sally?' Poppy queried.

'Yes...yes, it's this baby thing. She's got it into her head that she wants a baby,' he blurted out. 'She knew when we got married that... I'm not like James. Of course I want a family, but not yet... I want to have Sally to myself for a while but she won't listen to me.'

'Oh, Chris, I'm so sorry,' Poppy sympathised. 'But it's Sally you should really be talking to about this,' she advised him gently, 'not me...'

It was odd how the boyish look which had once caught so painfully at her heart now just made her feel cousinly—motherly almost.

'Yes, I suppose you are right,' Chris agreed ruefully, adding warmly, 'It's good to see you and James so happy together, Poppy... You've always been special to me,' he added in a muffled voice, leaning forward to give her a fierce hug that took her breath away as well as her balance.

Neither of them heard the door open or saw James come in until he rasped, 'What the hell's going on here?'

It was Chris who answered him, apparently oblivious to his fury and Poppy's anxiety as he responded cheerfully, 'Sorry, James; I just came round to have a chat with Poppy. I shan't forget what you said,' he told her, before glancing at his watch and announcing, 'I'd better get back; Sally will be wondering where I am.'

Poppy trembled as she saw the way James watched her as Chris closed the door and left.

'And what exactly was it that you said, that he won't forget?' he demanded menacingly. 'Or can I guess? Were you telling him how much you still love him, Poppy? How much you still want him?'

'No,' Poppy cried out in shocked protest. 'No, James, you've got it all wrong. It wasn't anything like that... Chris—'

'Don't lie to me, Poppy,' James interrupted her harshly. 'There isn't any point. We both know how you feel about Chris. How did you get him to come here? What did you tell him? That you wished he'd been the one you'd married, that he was the one you wanted when you lay in my arms—is that what you told him?'

'No,' Poppy denied, alarmed by the violence in his voice. 'No, of course not. James, you've—'

'No! What did you tell him? Did you tell him, perhaps, about the way you begged me to make love to you...about the way you pleaded with me to satisfy you?'

Poppy stared at him in shock. She had never seen him so angry, so out of control.

'My God, you couldn't wait long enough to make sure I was safely out of the way before you got him here, could you?' he demanded. 'How long has it been going on, Poppy? How often has he been coming round when I'm not here...?'

Suddenly Poppy had had enough, her shock giving way to pain as she retaliated bitterly, 'Why should *you* care? You're never here and—'

'And Chris, of course, is. What did you do to get him here—pretend you needed a cousin's shoulder to cry on? What exactly are you hoping for, Poppy? You know he doesn't want you.'

'Yes, I do,' she agreed starkly, her eyes registering her anguish as she mentally added, And, much more importantly, neither do you.

'Chris came here to talk to me about Sally,' she told James quietly, her anger subsiding under the weight of her pain. 'He's concerned because she wants to start a family when they'd agreed that they would wait for a while.'

'A family... Is that when you told him that she's not the only one to want his child...? Is *that* why he told you that you were very special to him...?'

Poppy couldn't conceal her small flush as he repeated the words Chris had said to her.

'Chris just came here for advice...as a cousin,' she told him shakily.

'A cousin! Is that why you were in his arms?' James asked sarcastically.

'James, where are you going?' Poppy protested as he pushed past her and into the hall.

'To get what I came back for,' he told her grimly.'Knowing how much you dislike coming home to find me here, I left in too much of a hurry and forgot some papers I need and so I had to come back for them.'

Poppy heard the door slam as he went into the small room he used as a study. She was still standing in the kitchen when he walked back in.

'James, we need to talk,' she told him bravely. 'We can't go on like this.'

'So what do you suggest we do? Get a divorce?' he demanded savagely. 'Get out of my way, Poppy,' he advised her angrily, 'before I do something we'll both regret.' He paused in the doorway to turn round and tell her brutally, 'And I warn you now, if you do ever find a way of persuading my brother to fulfil those adolescent fantasies of yours, I promise I'll make the pair of you sorry you were ever born. You don't really love him, Poppy; you don't *know* what real love is.'

No, I don't love him, Poppy agreed silently, listening to the engine of his car fire as he started it, the tears pouring down her face. I love you.

And, as for real love, she knew what it was to feel it but she certainly didn't know what it was like to receive it. 'What do you suggest we do?' James had challenged her. 'Get a divorce?' Did that mean that he was regretting their marriage, that he wanted to bring it to an end?

Unable to endure the loneliness of her own home, Poppy spent the rest of the weekend with her parents, explaining away her pale face and preoccupied manner by admitting wanly that she was missing James, which was, after all, the truth—or at least part of it.

On Monday morning, although she had a splitting headache, brought on, she suspected, by having spent half the night crying into her pillow, she insisted on going into work despite her mother's suggestion that she stay at home, but by mid-morning the pain in her head had become so intense that she finally gave in and told Chris that she intended to go home.

'You can't drive,' Chris told her after one look at her too pale face. 'I'll take you. When is James due home?'

Poppy turned away, unwilling to admit that she didn't know. She could have found out easily enough, she assumed, by asking his secretary but her pride wouldn't allow her to betray how little she knew about her husband's movements.

Chris had just pulled out onto the main road when it happened. He had to stop to avoid a cyclist and the driver of the car behind them didn't realise what had happened in time and ran into the back of them.

Poppy felt the impact jerk her forward in her seat against the restraint of her seat belt, automatically crying out both against the sharp, searing agony and in fear for her baby, the pain catapulting her into a pit of smothering darkness as she slid into a deep faint.

The first thing she heard when she came round was the sound of an ambulance, although she didn't realise then that it was coming for her.

'Don't move, Poppy,' Chris urged her anxiously as she tried to struggle against the restraining belt.

At some point he must have got out of the car, Poppy recognised, because he was now standing beside the open passenger door, whilst another man, a stranger, peered in at her and blustered defensively, 'It was only a little bit of a knock... Can't have done that much damage.'

'She's pregnant,' she heard Chris hiss angrily back. 'My God, man, why the hell couldn't you have watched what you were doing?'

'Damn cyclist.' The man crumpled. 'It was all his fault.'

'I doubt that the police will see it that way,' Chris warned him grimly.

Poppy wished they would both go away and stop arguing. The sound of their voices was making her head hurt and she dared not even think about what that agonisingly sharp pain she could feel in her body might portend.

'James... James... where are you...?'

She didn't even know she had said the words out loud until the driver of the other car asked, 'Who's this James?'

'Her husband,' Chris told him sharply. 'And I wouldn't want to be in your shoes when he finds out what's happened.'

Poppy was shaking with shock by the time the police car and the ambulance finally arrived.

'Sorry, love,' the ambulanceman apologised as he gently helped Poppy from the car, refusing to let her walk, insisting she get on the stretcher instead. 'It's these roadworks, see; we couldn't get through them.'

'What happened exactly?' Poppy heard him asking Chris, and she could see the way he frowned when the policeman muttered something to him about the car having been pushed along the road for quite some distance.

However, there was only calm reassurance in his eyes as he turned back to Poppy and told her gently, 'Best get you where they can take a proper look at you, love.'

'I'll come with you...' Chris began, but Poppy shook her head.

'No... There's no need; I don't want you,' she told Chris huskily. 'I want James...' Her eyes filled with tears she couldn't control, her whole body shaking with them.

Never mind me; what about my baby? she wanted to scream as the ambulanceman asked her if she was in any pain anywhere. The sharp pain she had felt before had subsided but the baby was ominously still and Poppy, who had felt exasperated some nights when she had been kept awake by its kicking, prayed desperately now for it to move.

The drive to the hospital seemed to take for ever and Poppy saw the concerned looks that the two ambulancemen exchanged when she was sick twice on the way there. The nurse who admitted her was kind as well as efficient, promising to get in touch with Poppy's parents and assuring her at the same time that babies were tougher than one thought.

'Let's get you sorted out first,' she told Poppy, adding, 'That's a nasty bump you've got on your forehead . . . does it hurt?'

Poppy, who hadn't even realised until then that she had bumped her head, touched her temple and winced as her fingers came away sticky with blood.

By the time her mother and father arrived she was tucked up in bed.

'Oh, darling . . . how do you feel?' her mother asked her anxiously as she hurried to her side.

'I'm all right,' Poppy assured her. 'It's the baby.'

She saw the look her parents exchanged and her anxiety increased.

'They keep telling me not to worry . . . that it's best to rest . . . but I haven't felt her kick for ages and I had this awful pain. I want James,' she told her mother bleakly.

'Chris is doing his best to find him, darling,' her mother tried to reassure her. 'He'd left the people he was visiting before Chris could get in touch with him and we can't get through to him on his mobile phone.'

'He won't use it in the car,' Poppy told her fretfully. 'He says it's too dangerous.'

The afternoon passed in a haze of examinations and hushed conversations out of her earshot which left her feeling increasingly anxious. The baby still hadn't moved and she was growing afraid that something might have happened to it. To her . . . to James's child, James's daughter.

Fresh tears rolled down her face. Her parents had volunteered to stay with her but she had sent them home. It was James she wanted. Only James.

She closed her eyes, whispering his name, her hands folded protectively across her belly. If only she had been holding their baby like that earlier, it might not have been hurt, she thought miserably.

She tensed as the door of her room opened, but it wasn't James who came in.

'Chris,' she said weakly in disappointment, subsiding back against the pillows. 'Where's James? Have you been able to contact him?'

'Not yet.' He tried to smile, but Poppy could see how anxious he was. 'Don't worry.'

He tried to comfort her, taking hold of her hand and patting it, but, weak from shock and fear, Poppy snatched it back, telling him crossly, 'Don't . . . don't; it isn't you I want, it's James.' As she started to cry harder she was distantly aware of Chris ringing the bell for the nurse and of her suddenly appearing and the two of them talking in lowered voices. She strained to hear what they were saying.

'She wants her husband,' the nurse told Chris. 'She's in a very unstable condition, and we're rather concerned about the foetal heartbeat . . .'

'We're doing our best to find him,' she heard Chris respond. 'He should have been back by now. God knows where the hell he is,' he added feelingly.

Poppy closed her eyes. James had gone; he didn't care about what happened to her. If anything should happen to their baby, he wouldn't even know and she would have lost them both. Without them, what was the point in her going on? She could hardly swallow past the huge lump of misery blocking her throat.

'They want me to go now,' she heard Chris telling her awkwardly as he responded to the nurse's brief nod and stood up.

Poppy didn't care if he stayed or went. Without James she was alone anyway, would always be alone.

At some point she must have drifted off to sleep. She knew that the nurse had administered some kind of sedative—'to rest the baby', she had told Poppy firmly when she had tried to object.

Now, as she opened her eyes, she realised that the headache and sickness that she had felt earlier had gone but that her body felt stiff and sore and the graze on her temple throbbed painfully.

The room was in darkness, but as she turned her head she realised that Chris was there, standing just inside the door, and that his arrival was probably the reason why she had woken up.

'Poppy...' Chris began, but Poppy turned her head away from him.

'Go away, Chris,' she told him quietly.

As she heard the door close behind him she let out a small sob.

'James...James, where are you? I love you so much,' she whispered under her breath. 'I love you both so much,' she added as she touched the still bump of her stomach. 'James...'

'Yes, Poppy, I'm here.'

The shock of hearing his voice made her stiffen and then turn her head so quickly that she winced in sudden pain.

'James!' she repeated in disbelief, her eyes fastening hungrily on his shadowy outline in the darkness, as though she was afraid to believe that he was actually there. 'When...? How...?' she began, trembling as he sat down next to her.

'Chris had left a message for me at home,' he told her sombrely, then emotion broke through the controlled tautness of his voice as he exploded, 'My God, Poppy, how—?'

'It wasn't Chris's fault,' she told him quickly. 'It was an accident; he...' She had started to shake violently, her finger picking anxiously at the coverlet until James reached out and took hold of her.

'You're cold,' he said, but Poppy shook her head, dismissing her own injuries as she told him quickly, 'James, it's our baby... I can't feel her kicking any more. They keep telling me not to worry and that she's all right... but how can she be all right when she's so still? Oh, James, I'm so afraid for her,' she whispered helplessly. 'She's so small, so vulnerable and I love her so much.'

'Chris said that you told him to go away, that you only wanted me. Is that true?' James asked huskily.

'Yes,' Poppy admitted, and raised her head off the pillow to ask him uncertainly, 'Where were you?'

'On my way to Italy... to the villa.'

'What...? Why?'

'You are not the only one to indulge in pointless fantasies, you know,' James told her obliquely. 'The only difference between us is that I've had a hell of a lot more experience at doing it.'

'Fantasies? What fantasies?' Poppy demanded uncertainly.

'Oh, the usual kind,' James told her gravely. 'That the woman I love loves me back, that she wants me, that in the darkness of the night, in the privacy of our shared bed, she turns to me and tells me that she aches for me to touch her, to love her and to go on loving her for ever.'

As she listened to him, Poppy's body started to stiffen in anguished shock.

'Who is she...this woman?' she asked shakily.
James was in love with someone else. Why had she
never guessed...realised...? 'Do I know her?'

'Yes, you know her,' James admitted, but he wasn't
looking at her any longer, Poppy recognised. He was
looking at her body instead.

'The baby!' she suddenly gasped in delight. 'She's
moving... Oh, James, she's moving, she's all right,
she's...' Even now Poppy couldn't bring herself to
say the word 'alive' and to admit by saying it just
what she had been dreading. 'Oh, James.' As she
clutched his hand, happy tears poured down her face.

'Why did you want me with you and not Chris,
Poppy?' James asked her as he reached out his hand
and covered the small bulge.

'You're...you're my husband,' Poppy told him,
unable to bring herself to look properly at him. 'My
baby's—our baby's—father and...'

'And?' James prompted.

He wasn't looking at her. He was still looking at
her stomach, which was perhaps why she suddenly
found the courage to tell him.

'And because I love you,' Poppy admitted quietly.
'But I know that isn't what you want,' she added
hastily. 'I'm not an adolescent any more, James. I do
know now what truly loving someone means. If you
want me to...to set you free so that you can go to
her...to the woman you love...then I'll...' she said
bravely, then stopped to bite down hard on her bottom
lip as her emotion threatened to overwhelm her.

'Go to her? I'm already with her,' James told
her softly.

'Already with her?' Poppy's heart started to thump heavily as she looked indignantly from the closed door to his face. 'You've brought her here ... now ...?'

'Oh, Poppy.' Suddenly, unbearably, he was actually laughing at her—laughing as he stood up and then leaned over the bed, gathering her up in his arms to hold her close and touch her tenderly.

'You're the one I love, the one I've always loved. Are you really so blind that you never knew it?'

'You love me ...? But you can't,' she protested. 'You've always been so angry with me, so I—'

'Because that was the only way I had of defending myself, protecting myself from the pain of knowing that you only had eyes for Chris. I fell in love with you about the same time that you fell in love with him.'

'But if you love me, why—?' Poppy stopped, her face suddenly crimsoning.

'Why what?' James pressed.

'Why did you act the way you did after ... after ...? Why did you behave so coldly to me after we'd made love?' she asked him huskily. 'You must have known how much I wanted you.' Her colour deepened. 'I thought you were ... I thought you didn't want me any more, that I'd disgusted you—'

'Disgusted me?' James interrupted her. 'Oh, Poppy, if only you knew what it did to me when you told me that you wanted me. You'll never know how close I came that night to telling you how I felt, but I couldn't get out of my mind the way you'd told me that you wanted me to be Chris ... that you'd believed that first time that I *was* Chris.

'I stopped being intimate with you because I had no choice. I knew that it was only a matter of time before my control broke and I told you how I felt and I couldn't lay that burden on you. Not after everything else I'd done.'

'Everything else ... What else?' Poppy demanded.

'Making love to you when I knew you couldn't really want me ... when I knew that you were still a virgin and unlikely to be using any form of birth control ... and, having done so once, being unable to resist repeating the offence and knowing when I did how it increased the likelihood that you would conceive.'

'I think I knew I had,' Poppy told him in awe, before admitting half-shyly, 'There was something—a feeling, a sort of knowing.'

'I didn't set out to force you into a position where you'd have to marry me,' James told her, 'but, once I knew the possibility was there, there was no way I was not going to use it. I told myself that it was me who'd made love to you, me your body wanted, even if your heart remained locked against me, and that somehow I'd find a way of making you see that you couldn't possibly want me so much physically without there being some possibility that you might come to love me.'

'I probably already loved you, even before ... before we made love,' Poppy told him hesitantly. 'When I was young ... Before ... You were always ... It was *you* I loved best then,' she told him softly, 'but somehow when I started to grow up ...'

'Everyone goes through teenage crushes,' James told her gently.

'I can't understand how I ever thought that what I felt for Chris was really love,' Poppy said. 'When I look back now ...'

She stopped talking as James bent his head and kissed her.

'James...? James?' she demanded, shaking his arm as she broke the kiss.

'What is it?'

'I want to go home,' she told him unsteadily. 'Please make them let me go home...with you...'

'Are you sure?' James asked her quietly, searching her face and then cupping it in his hands to kiss her—holding her as though he simply couldn't bear to let her go, Poppy recognised with a sense of wonder.

Now that she knew the truth it amazed her that she had not seen it for herself. The love she had thought could never be hers was there, displayed in his every touch, his every look. It wasn't just with words that love was communicated, Poppy knew with sudden wisdom.

Looking back, she could see that it was perhaps no wonder that she had responded physically to James the way she had that first time they had made love; her body had recognised the truth that her mind had been too stubborn and perhaps a little too immature to want to see. There was no point in even trying to compare what she felt for James with the feelings she had had for Chris.

Chris!

She gave James a rueful look.

'I was horrid to poor Chris,' she told him solemnly.

'Good,' James replied unsympathetically, and then relented to smile lovingly at her.

'Do you think things will be all right with him and Sally,' Poppy asked him anxiously, 'now that she's decided she wants a baby?'

'Chris and Sally love one another; there's no doubt about that. They'll find a way of working things out.'

'I'm so glad you're here,' Poppy whispered as he bent his head to kiss her again. 'And so,' she added, 'is your daughter. Oh, James—' she clung to him, trembling slightly '—if anything had happened...'

'Don't,' he begged her. 'If anything happened to you, I don't think I could bear to go on living.'

The nurse clicked her tongue reprovingly when she came into the room and found her patient wrapped in her husband's arms.

'I want to go home,' Poppy told her.

'Well, I don't know about that,' she said disapprovingly. 'You're supposed to be resting...'

The doctor, however, when summoned by James, took a more benign view. There was no reason why Poppy shouldn't go home, just so long as she took things easy for a few days, he declared.

'Don't worry...she will,' James assured him, adding in an undertone to Poppy, his face mock-severe, 'Even if I have to stay in bed with her to make her do so...'

'No more business trips away from home?' Poppy questioned James some twenty minutes later as he gently helped her into his car.

'None,' he assured her firmly. 'From now on Chris can handle those.'

'Poor Sally,' Poppy protested.

'Well, perhaps not all of them,' James allowed. 'But the only way I shall be working away from home in future is if my wife comes with me.'

'There's just one condition,' Poppy told him mockingly.

'And that is?' James demanded, his eyebrows lifting in a return of his old hauteur.

'That the head of the company and his translator get to share a double room, and a double bed,' Poppy purred. 'All in the name of financial economy, of course.'

'Of course,' James agreed, and then added in a husky voice as he saw the way Poppy was looking at him, 'You're supposed to be resting—remember?'

EPILOGUE

HOLLY JOY was born four days before Christmas, just in time for her already doting father to take her and her mother home with him to spend their first Christmas together as a family.

'She's perfect,' James told Poppy lovingly on Christmas Eve as he watched her feeding their small daughter. 'But not as perfect as you.'

Poppy laughed.

'I can remember a time when "perfect" was the last adjective you would have used to describe me,' she reminded him. She laughed again as Holly Joy squeaked her protest at having her enjoyment of her supper disrupted by her father's determination to kiss her mother but that laughter was soon stilled as she responded to the love and passion she could feel in James's kiss.

'Do you realise that I wanted our baby to be a girl because I saw it as a way of loving a miniature version of you?' he murmured, and Poppy, listening to his confession, felt tears forming as she understood just how much her husband wanted—had always wanted—her love.

Around her neck she was wearing the creamy pearls which James had given her to celebrate their baby's birth, and amongst the presents which had arrived for Holly Joy from her aunt Sally had been a handmade silver bracelet in an unusual design of flowers and ribbons, rather like a bridal wreath.

Poppy had also received from her a bouquet of flowers which she'd instantly recognised. How long ago it seemed now since she had caught Sally's wedding bouquet and yet, in reality, it was barely ten months.

'It didn't seem appropriate to send you this when you and James married; I don't know why,' Sally had written on the accompanying card. 'But now it does. Two down, one to go...'

Poppy laughed as she showed James the card.

'Well, she may have got her way with me,' she told him, 'but she's not going to find it so easy with Star. She really is anti-marriage and anti-commitment. Still, two out of three isn't bad.'

'Mmm,' James murmured, gathering her in his arms after she had put Holly back in her cot. 'Right now I've got far more interesting things I want to do than talk about Sally's manipulation of superstition.'

'Such as?' Poppy teased.

'Come here and let me show you...'

Laughingly she did.

If you are looking for more titles by
PENNY JORDAN
Don't miss these fabulous stories by one of
Harlequin's most popular authors:

Take 4 bestselling love stories FREE

Plus get a FREE surprise gift!

Special Limited-time Offer

Mail to Harlequin Reader Service®

3010 Walden Avenue
P.O. Box 1867
Buffalo, N.Y. 14240-1867

YES! Please send me 4 free Harlequin Presents® novels and my free surprise gift. Then send me 6 brand-new novels every month, which I will receive months before they appear in bookstores. Bill me at the low price of $2.90 each plus 25¢ delivery and applicable sales tax, if any*. That's the complete price and a savings of over 10% off the cover prices—quite a bargain! I understand that accepting the books and gift places me under no obligation ever to buy any books. I can always return a shipment and cancel at any time. Even if I never buy another book from Harlequin, the 4 free books and the surprise gift are mine to keep forever.

108 BPA A3UL

Name	(PLEASE PRINT)	
Address	Apt. No.	
City	State	Zip

This offer is limited to one order per household and not valid to present Harlequin Presents® subscribers. *Terms and prices are subject to change without notice. Sales tax applicable in N.Y.

Free Gift Offer

With a Free Gift proof-of-purchase
from any Harlequin® book, you can receive
a beautiful cubic zirconia pendant.

This stunning marquise-shaped stone is a genuine cubic
zirconia—accented by an 18" gold tone necklace.
(Approximate retail value $19.95)

Send for yours today...
compliments of ◈HARLEQUIN®

To receive your free gift, a cubic zirconia pendant, send us one original proof-of-purchase, photocopies not accepted, from the back of any Harlequin Romance®, Harlequin Presents®, Harlequin Temptation®, Harlequin Superromance®, Harlequin Intrigue®, Harlequin American Romance®, or Harlequin Historicals® title available at your favorite retail outlet, together with the Free Gift Certificate, plus a check or money order for $1.65 U.S./$2.15 CAN. (do not send cash) to cover postage and handling, payable to Harlequin Free Gift Offer. We will send you the specified gift. Allow 6 to 8 weeks for delivery. Offer good until December 31, 1997, or while quantities last. Offer valid in the U.S. and Canada only.

Free Gift Certificate

Name: _____

Address: _____

City: _____ State/Province: _____ Zip/Postal Code: _____

Mail this certificate, one proof-of-purchase and a check or money order for postage and handling to: HARLEQUIN FREE GIFT OFFER 1997. In the U.S.: 3010 Walden Avenue, P.O. Box 9071, Buffalo NY 14269-9057. In Canada: P.O. Box 604, Fort Erie, Ontario L2Z 5X3.

FREE GIFT OFFER   084-KEZ

ONE PROOF-OF-PURCHASE
To collect your fabulous FREE GIFT, a cubic zirconia pendant, you must include this original proof-of-purchase for each gift with the properly completed Free Gift Certificate.

084-KEZR